FAIRY TALES FROM SWEDISH

CW00641196

"TWIGMUNTUS, COWBELLIANTUS, PERCHNOSIUS? CAN YOU GIVE ME AN
ANSWER TO THAT?" THE LAD ASKED.

FAIRY TALES

FROM THE SWEDISH

OF

BARON G. DJURKLOU

TRANSLATED BY

H. L. BRÆKSTAD

WITH ILLUSTRATIONS BY

TH. KITTELSEN & ERIK WERENSKIOLD

AND A FRONTISPIECE BY CARL LARSSON

1901

LIST OF ILLUSTRATIONS

SHOUTED THE WOMAN

"NO, KEEP AWAY FROM ME!" CRIED OLD NICK, AND KEPT HER BACK WITH HIS POLE

JUST THEN TWO WHITE PIGEONS CAME FLYING OUT OF THE COTTAGE...THEY WERE THE MAN AND HIS WIFE

"CLUCK! CLUCK!" SHE CRIED, AND WANTED TO GET AWAY

BUSINESS WAS SO BRISK, THAT IT WAS AS MUCH AS HE COULD DO TO GET OUT HIS STUFF AND MEASURE WHAT THEY WANTED

THE PEDLAR OPENED THE BAG, AND WHO SHOULD PEEP OUT BUT KATIE GREY!

"FOR, AFTER ALL, IT'S HARD TO DIE ON AN EMPTY STOMACH," SAID THE EXECUTIONER

TRANSLATOR'S NOTE

The interesting and characteristic collection of Swedish Folk and Fairy Tales published by Baron Djurklou nearly twenty years ago, has, strange to say, escaped the attention of folk-lorists outside the country of their origin. They are written in the dialect of the Swedish peasantry, to the study of which the author has devoted so much time and labour, and they may therefore have presented difficulties in the way of translation into other languages. In the present English version of a selection from the tales the translator has tried to retain as far as possible the humorous and colloquial style of the original. The illustrations in the body of the book are by T. Kittelsen and E. Werenskiold, two well-known Norwegian artists, and the frontispiece is by Carl Larsson, the prince of Swedish illustrators.

H. L. B.

"LARS, MY LAD!"

There was once a prince or a duke, or something of that sort, but at any rate he belonged to a very grand family, and he would not stop at home. So he travelled all over the world, and wherever he went he was well liked, and was received in the best and gayest families, for he had no end of money. He made friends and acquaintances, as you may imagine, wherever he went, for he who has a well-filled trough is sure to fall in with pigs who want to have their fill. But he went on spending his money until he came to want, and at last his purse became so empty that he had not even a farthing left. And now there was an end to all his friends as well, for they behaved like the pigs; when the trough was empty and he had no more to give them, they began to grunt and grin, and then they ran away in all directions. There he stood alone with a long face. Everybody had been so willing to help him to get rid of his money, but nobody would help him in return; and so there was nothing for it but to trudge home and beg for crusts on the way.

So late one evening he came to a great forest. He did not know where he should find a shelter for the night, but he went on looking and searching till he caught sight of an old tumble-down hut, which stood in the middle of some bushes. It was not exactly good enough for such a fine cavalier, but when you cannot get what you want you must take what you can get. And, since there was no help for it, he went into the hut. Not a living soul was to be seen; there was not even a stool to sit upon, but alongside the wall stood a big chest. What could there be inside that chest? If only there were some bits of mouldy bread in it! How nice they would taste! For, you must know, he had not had a single bit of food the whole day, and he was so hungry and his stomach so empty that it groaned with pain. He lifted the lid. But inside the chest there was another chest, and inside that chest there was another; and so it went on, each one smaller than the other, until they became quite tiny boxes. The more there were the harder he worked away, for there must be something very fine inside, he thought, since it was so well hidden.

At last he came to a tiny, little box, and in this box lay a bit of paper—and that was all he got for his trouble! It was very annoying, of course, but then he discovered there was something written on the paper, and

8

when he looked at it he was just able to spell it out, although at first it looked somewhat difficult.

"Lars, my lad!"

As he pronounced these words something answered right in his ear:

"What are master's orders?"

He looked round, but he saw nobody. This was very funny, he thought, and so he read out the words once more:

"Lars, my lad!"

And the answer came as before:

"What are master's orders?"

But he did not see anybody this time either.

"If there is anybody about who hears what I say, then be kind enough to bring me something to eat," he said. And the next moment there stood a table laid out with all the best things one could think of. He set to work to eat and drink, and had a proper fill. He had never enjoyed himself so much in all his life, he thought.

When he had eaten all he could get down, he began to feel sleepy, and so he took out the paper again:

"Lars, my lad!"

"What are master's orders?"

"Well, you have given me food and drink, and now you must get me a bed to sleep in as well. But I want a really fine bed," he said, for you must know he was a little more bold now that his hunger was stayed. Well, there it stood, a bed so fine and dainty that even the king himself might covet it. Now this was all very well in its way; but when once you are well off you wish for still more, and he had no sooner got into bed than he began to think that the room was altogether too wretched for such a grand bed. So he took out the paper again:

"Lars, my lad!"

"What are master's orders?"

"Since you are able to get me such food and such a bed here in the midst of the wild forest, I suppose you can manage to get me a better

9

room, for you see I am accustomed to sleep in a palace, with golden mirrors and draped walls and ornaments and comforts of all kinds," he said. Well, he had no sooner spoken the words than he found himself lying in the grandest chamber anybody had ever seen.

Now he was comfortable, he thought, and felt quite satisfied as he turned his face to the wall and closed his eyes.

But that was not all the grandeur; for when he woke up in the morning and looked round, he saw it was a big palace he had been sleeping in. One room led into the other, and wherever he went the place was full of all sorts of finery and luxuries, both on the walls and on the ceilings, and they glittered so much when the sun shone on them, that he had to shade his eyes with his hand, so strong was the glare of gold and silver wherever he turned. He then happened to look out of the window. Good gracious! How grand it was! There was something else than pine forests and juniper bushes to look at, for there was the finest garden any one could wish for, with splendid trees and roses of all kinds. But he could not see a single human being, or even a cat; and that, you know, was rather lonely, for otherwise he had everything so grand and had been set up as his own master again.

So he took out the bit of paper:

"Lars, my lad!"

"What are master's orders?"

"Well now you have given me food and bed and a palace to live in, and I intend to remain here, for I like the place," he said, "yet I don't like to live quite by myself. I must have both lads and lasses whom I may order about to wait upon me," he said.

And there they were. There came servants and stewards and scullery maids and chambermaids of all sorts, and some came bowing and some curtseying. So now the duke thought he was really satisfied.

But now it happened that there was a large palace on the other side of the forest, and there the king lived who owned the forest, and the great, big fields around it. As he was walking up and down in his room he happened to look out through the window and saw the new palace, where the golden weathercocks were swinging to and fro on the roof in the sunlight, which dazzled his eyes.

"This is very strange," he thought; and so he called his courtiers. They came rushing in, and began bowing and scraping.

"Do you see the palace over there?" said the king.

They opened their eyes and began to stare.

Yes, of course they saw it.

"Who is it that has dared to build such a palace in my grounds?" said the king.

They bowed, and they scraped with their feet, but they did not know anything about it.

The king then called his generals and captains.

They came, stood to attention and presented arms.

"Be gone, soldiers and troopers," said the king, "and pull down the palace over there, and hang him who has built it; and don't lose any time about it!"

Well, they set off in great haste to arm themselves, and away they went. The drummers beat the skins of their drums, and the trumpeters blew their trumpets, and the other musicians played and blew as best they could, so that the duke heard them long before he could see them. But he had heard that kind of noise before, and knew what it meant, so he took out his scrap of paper:

"Lars, my lad!"

"What are master's orders?"

"There are soldiers coming here," he said, "and now you must provide me with soldiers and horses, that I may have double as many as those over in the wood, and with sabres and pistols, and guns and cannons with all that belongs to them; but be quick about it."

"DO YOU SEE THE PALACE OVER THERE?" SAID THE KING.

And no time was lost; for when the duke looked out, he saw an immense number of soldiers, who were drawn up around the palace.

When the king's men arrived, they came to a sudden halt and dared not advance. But the duke was not afraid; he went straight up to the colonel of the king's soldiers and asked him what he wanted.

The colonel told him his errand.

"It's of no use," said the duke. "You see how many men I have; and if the king will listen to me, we shall become good friends, and I will help him against his enemies, and in such a way that it will be heard of far and wide," he said.

The colonel was of the same opinion, and the duke then invited him and all his soldiers inside the palace, and the men had more than one glass to drink and plenty of everything to eat as well.

But while they were eating and drinking they began talking; and the duke then got to hear that the king had a daughter who was his only child, and was so wonderfully fair and beautiful that no one had ever seen her like before. And the more the king's soldiers ate and drank the more they thought she would suit the duke for a wife.

And they went on talking so long that the duke at last began to be of the same opinion. "The worst of it," said the soldiers, "is that she is just as proud as she is beautiful, and will never look at a man."

But the duke laughed at this. "If that's all," said the duke, "there's sure to be a remedy for that complaint."

When the soldiers had eaten and drunk as much as they could find room for, they shouted "Hurrah!" so that it echoed among the hills, and then they set out homewards. But, as you may imagine, they did not walk exactly in parade order, for they were rather unsteady about the knees, and many of them did not carry their guns in regulation manner. The duke asked them to greet the king from him. He would call on him the following day, he said.

When the duke was alone again, he began to think of the princess, and to wonder if she were as beautiful and fair as they had made her out to be. He would like to make sure of it; and as so many strange things had happened that day that it might not be impossible to find that out as well, he thought.

"Lars, my lad!"

"What are master's orders?"

"Well, now you must bring me the king's daughter as soon as she has gone to sleep," he said; "but she must not be awakened either on the way here or back. Do you hear that?" he said. And before long the princess was lying on the bed. She slept so soundly and looked so wonderfully beautiful, as she lay there. Yes, she was as sweet as sugar, I can tell you.

The duke walked round about her, but she was just as beautiful from whatever point of view he looked at her.

The more he looked the more he liked her.

"Lars, my lad!"

"What are master's orders?"

"You must now carry the princess home," he said, "for now I know how she looks, and to-morrow I will ask for her hand," he said.

Next morning the king looked out of the window. "I suppose I shall not be troubled with the sight of that palace any more," he thought. But, zounds! There it stood just as on the day before, and the sun shone so brightly on the roof, and the weathercocks dazzled his eyes.

He now became furious, and called all his men.

They came quicker than usual.

The courtiers bowed and scraped, and the soldiers stood to attention and presented arms.

"Do you see the palace there?" screamed the king.

They stretched their necks, and stared and gaped.

Yes, of course, that they did.

"Have I not ordered you to pull down the palace and hang the builder?" he said.

Yes, they could not deny that; but then the colonel himself stepped forward and reported what had happened and how many soldiers the duke had, and how wonderfully grand the palace was.

And next he told him what the duke had said, and how he had asked him to give his greetings to the king, and all that sort of thing.

The king felt quite confused, and had to put his crown on the table and scratch his head. He could not understand all this, although he was a king; for he could take his oath it had all been built in a single night; and if the duke were not the evil one himself, he must in any case have done it by magic.

While he sat there pondering, the princess came into the room.

"Good morning to you, father!" she said. "Just fancy, I had such a strange and beautiful dream last night!" she said.

"What did you dream then, my girl?" said the king.

"I dreamt I was in the new palace over yonder, and that I saw a duke there, so fine and handsome that I could never have imagined the like; and now I want to get married, father," she said.

"Do you want to get married? you, who never cared to look at a man! That's very strange!" said the king.

"That may be," said the princess; "but it's different now, and I want to get married, and it's the duke I want," she said.

The king was quite beside himself, so frightened did he become of the duke.

But all of a sudden he heard a terrible noise of drums and trumpets and instruments of all kinds; and then came a message that the duke had just arrived with a large company, all of whom were so grandly dressed that gold and silver glistened in every fold. The king put on his crown and his coronation robes, and then went out on the steps to receive them. And the princess was not slow to follow him.

The duke bowed most graciously, and the king of course did likewise, and when they had talked a while about their affairs and their grandeur they became the best of friends. A great banquet was then prepared, and the duke was placed next to the princess at the table. What they talked about is not easy to tell, but the duke spoke so well for himself that the princess could not very well say "no" to anything he said, and then he went up to the king and asked for her hand. The king could not exactly say "no" either, for he could very well see that the duke was a person with whom it were best to be on friendly terms; but give his sanction there and then, he could not very well do that either. He wanted to see the duke's palace first, and find out about the state of affairs over there, as you may understand.

So it was arranged that he should visit the duke and take the princess with him to see his palace; and with this they parted company.

When the duke returned home, Lars became busier than ever, for there was so much to attend to. But he set to work and strove hard; and when the king and his daughter arrived everything was so magnificent and splendid that no words can describe it. They went through all the rooms and looked about, and they found everything as it should be, and even still more splendid, thought the king, and so he was quite pleased.

The wedding then took place, and that in grand style; and on the duke's arrival home with his bride he too gave a great feast, and then there was an end to the festivities.

Some time passed by, and one evening the duke heard these words:

"Are you satisfied now?"

It was Lars, as you may guess, but the duke could not see him.

"Well, I ought to be," said the duke. "You have provided me with everything I have," he said.

"Yes, but what have I got in return?" asked Lars.

"Nothing," said the duke; "but, bless me, what could I have given you, who are not of flesh and blood, and whom I cannot see either?" he said. "But if there is anything I can do for you, tell me what it is, and I shall do it."

"Well, I should like to ask you for that little scrap of paper which you found in the chest," said Lars.

"Nothing else?" said the duke. "If such a trifle can help you, I can easily do without it, for now I begin to know the words by heart," he said.

Lars thanked the duke, and asked him to put the paper on the chair in front of the bed, when he retired to rest, and he would be sure to fetch it during the night.

The duke did as he was told; and so he and the princess lay down and went to sleep.

But early in the morning the duke awoke and felt so cold that his teeth chattered, and when he had got his eyes quite open he found he was quite naked and had not even as much as a thread on his back; and instead of the grand bed and the beautiful bedroom, and the magnificent palace, he lay on the big chest in the old tumble-down hut.

He began to shout:

"Lars, my lad!" But he got no answer. He shouted once more:

"Lars, my lad!" But he got no answer this time either. So he shouted all he could:

"Lars, my lad!" But it was all in vain.

Now he began to understand how matters stood. When Lars had got the scrap of paper he was freed from service at the same time, and now he had taken everything with him. But there was no help for it. There stood the duke in the old hut quite naked; and as for the princess she was not much better off, although she had her clothes on, for she had got them from her father, so Lars had no power over them.

The duke had now to tell the princess everything, and ask her to leave him. He would have to manage as best he could, he said. But she would not hear of it. She well remembered what the parson had said when he married them, and she would never, never leave him, she said.

In the meantime the king in his palace had also awakened, and when he looked out of the window he did not see any sign whatever of the other palace, where his daughter and son-in-law lived. He became uneasy, as you may imagine, and called his courtiers.

They came in, and began to bow and scrape.

"Do you see the palace over yonder behind the forest?" he asked.

They stretched their necks and stared with all their might.

No, they did not see it.

"Where has it gone to, then?" asked the king.

Well, really they did not know.

It was not long before the king had set out with all his court through the forest; and when he arrived at the place where the palace with the beautiful gardens should have been, he could not see anything but heather and juniper bushes and firs. But then he discovered the old tumble-down hut, which stood there among the bushes. He entered the hut and—mercy on us!—what a sight met his eyes! There stood his son-in-law, quite naked, and his daughter, who had not very many clothes on either, and who was crying and moaning.

"Dear, dear! what does all this mean?" said the king; but he did not get any answer, for the duke would rather have died than tell him.

The king did his utmost to get him to speak; but in spite of all the king's promises and threats the duke remained obstinate and would not utter a word.

The king then became angry—and no wonder, for now he could see that this grand duke was not what he pretended to be, and so he ordered the duke to be hanged, and that without any loss of time. The princess begged and prayed for mercy; but neither prayers nor tears were of any help now; for an impostor he was, and as an impostor he should die, said the king.

And so it had to be. They erected a gallows, and placed the rope round the duke's neck. But while they were getting the gallows ready, the princess got hold of the hangman, and gave both him and his assistant some money, that they should so manage the hanging of the duke that he should not lose his life, and in the night they were to cut him down, so that he and the princess might then flee the country. And that's how the matter was arranged.

In the meantime they had strung up the duke, and the king and his court and all the people went their way.

The duke was now in great straits. He had, however, plenty of time to reflect how foolish he had been in not saving some of the crumbs when he was living in plenty, and how unpardonably stupid he had been in letting Lars have the scrap of paper. This vexed him more than all. If only he had it again, he thought, they should see he had been gaining some sense in return for all he had lost. But it is of little use snarling if you haven't got any teeth. "Ah, well, well!" he sighed, and so he dangled his legs, which was really all he could do.

The day passed slowly and tediously for him, and he was not at all displeased when he saw the sun setting behind the forest. But just before it disappeared he heard a fearful shouting, and when he looked down the hill, he saw seven cart-loads of worn-out shoes, and on the top of the hindmost cart he saw a little old man in grey clothes and with a red pointed cap on his head. His face was like that of the worst scarecrow, and the rest of him was not very handsome either.

He drove straight up to the gallows, and when he arrived right under it he stopped and looked up at the duke, and then burst out laughing, the ugly old fellow!

"I WONDER IF YOU CAN READ THIS?" SAID LARS, HOLDING
UP THE PAPER BEFORE THE DUKE'S EYES.

"How stupid you were!" he said; "but what should the fool do with his
stupidity if he did not make use of it?" And then he laughed again.
"Yes, there you are hanging now, and here am I carting away all the
shoes I have worn out for your whims. I wonder if you can read what

is written on this bit of paper, and if you recognise it?" he said with an ugly laugh, holding up the paper before the duke's eyes.

But all who hang are not dead, and this time it was Lars who was befooled.

The duke made a clutch, and snatched the paper from him.

"Lars, my lad!"

"What are master's orders?"

"Well, you must cut me down from the gallows and put the palace and all the rest in its place again, exactly as it was before, and when the night has set in you must bring back the princess."

All went merrily as in a dance, and before long everything was in its place, just as it was when Lars took himself off.

When the king awoke the next morning he looked out of the window, as was his custom, and there stood the palace again, with the weathercocks glittering so beautifully in the sunshine. He called his courtiers, and they came and began to bow and scrape.

They stretched their necks as far as they could, and stared and gaped.

"Do you see the palace over there?" said the king.

Yes, of course they did.

The king then sent for the princess, but she was not to be found. He then went out to see if his son-in-law was still hanging on the gallows, but neither son-in-law nor gallows was to be seen.

He had to lift off his crown and scratch his head. But that did not improve matters; he could not make head or tail of either one thing or the other. He set off at once with all his court through the forest, and when he came to the place where the palace should stand, there it stood sure enough. The gardens and the roses were exactly as they used to be, and the duke's people were to be seen everywhere among the trees. His son-in-law and his daughter received him on the steps, dressed in their finest clothes.

"Well, I never saw the like of this," said the king to himself; he could scarcely believe his own eyes, so wonderful did it all seem to him.

"God's peace be with you, father, and welcome here!" said the duke.

The king stood staring at him.

"Are you my son-in-law?" he asked.

"Well, I suppose I am," said the duke. "Who else should I be?"

"Did I not order you to be hanged yesterday like any common thief?" said the king.

"I think you must have been bewitched on the way," said the duke, with a laugh. "Do you think I am the man to let myself be hanged? Or is there any one here who dares to believe it?" he said, and looked so fiercely at the courtiers that they felt as if they were being pierced through and through.

They bowed and scraped and cringed before him.

"Who could believe such a thing? Was it at all likely?"

"Well, if there is any one who dares to say the king could have wished me such evil, let him speak out," said the duke, and fixed his eyes upon them still more fiercely than before.

They went on bowing and scraping and cringing.

How could any one dare to say such a thing? No, they had more sense than that, they should hope.

The king did not know what to believe, for when he looked at the duke he thought he never could have wished him such evil; but still he was not quite convinced.

"Did I not come here yesterday, and was not the whole palace gone, and was there not an old hut in its place? And did not I go into that hut, and did not you stand stark naked right before my eyes?" he asked.

"I wonder the king can talk so," said the duke. "I think the trolls must have bewitched your eyes in the forest and made you quite crazy; or what do you think?" he said, and turned round to the courtiers.

They bowed and bowed till their backs were bent double, and agreed with everything he said, there could be no mistake about that. The king rubbed his eyes, and looked round about him.

"I suppose it is as you say, then," he said to the duke, "and it is well I have got back my proper sight and have come to my senses again. For it would have been a sin and a shame if I had let you be hanged," he said; and so he was happy again, and nobody thought any more about the matter.

"Once bitten, twice shy," as the proverb says; and the duke now took upon himself to manage and look after most of his affairs, so that it was seldom Lars had to wear out his shoes. The king soon gave the duke half the kingdom into the bargain; so he had now plenty to do, and people said they would have to search a long time to find his equal in wise and just ruling.

Then one day Lars came to the duke, looking very little better than the first time he had seen him; but he was, of course, more humble, and did not dare to giggle and make grimaces.

"You do not want my help any longer, now," he said; "for although I did wear out my shoes at first, I am now unable to wear out a single pair, and my feet will soon be covered all over with moss. So I thought I might now get my leave of absence," he said.

The duke quite agreed with him. "I have tried to spare you, and I almost think I could do without you," he said. "But the palace and all the rest I do not want to lose, for such a clever builder as you I shall never get again; nor do I ever want to adorn the gallows again, as you can well understand; so I cannot give you back the paper on any account," he said.

LARS ON THE TRAMP.

"Well, as long as you have got it, I need not fear," said Lars; "but if anybody else should get hold of it there will be nothing but running and trudging about again, and that's what I want to avoid; for when one has been tramping about for a thousand years, as I have done, one begins to get tired of it," he said.

But they went on talking, and at last they agreed that the duke should put the paper in the box, and then bury it seven ells under the ground, under a stone fixed in the earth. They then thanked one another for the time they had spent in each other's company, and so they parted.

The duke carried out his part of the agreement, for he was not likely to want to change it. He lived happy and contented with the princess, and they had both sons and daughters. When the king died, he got the whole of the kingdom, and you may guess he was none the worse off for that; and there no doubt he still lives and reigns, if he is not dead.

But as for that box with the scrap of paper in it, there are many who are still running about looking for it.

THE SAUSAGE

There was once an old woman, who was all alone one evening in her cottage, occupied with her household affairs. While she was waiting for her husband, who was away at work over in the forest, and while she was bustling about, a fine, grand lady came in, and so the woman began to curtsey and curtsey, for she had never seen such a grand person before.

"I should be so much obliged if you would lend me your brewing pan," said the lady, "for my daughter is going to be married, and I expect guests from all parts."

Oh, dear, yes! That she might have, said the woman, although she could not remember whether she had ever seen her before, and so she went to fetch the pan.

The lady took it and thanked the woman, saying that she would pay her well for the loan of it, and so she went her way.

Two days afterwards the lady came back with it, and this time she also found the woman alone.

"Many thanks for the loan," said the lady, "and now in return you shall have three wishes."

And with this the lady left, and vanished so quickly that the old woman had not even time to ask her name or where she lived. But that did not matter, she thought, for now she had three wishes, and she began to think what she should wish for. She expected her husband back soon, and she thought it would be best to wait till he came home and could have a say in the matter. But the least they could wish for must be a fine big farm—the best in the parish, and a box full of money, and just fancy how happy and comfortable they would be then, for they had worked so hard all their days! Ah, yes, then the neighbours would have something to wonder at, for you may guess how they would stare at all the fine things she would have.

But since they were now so rich it was really a shame that there should be nothing but some blue, sour milk and some hard crusts of bread in the cupboard for her husband when he came home tired and weary, he who was fond of hot food. She had just been to her neighbour's, and there she had seen a fine big sausage, which they were going to have for supper.

"Ah, deary me, I wish I had that sausage here!" sighed the old woman; and the next moment a big sausage lay on the table right before her.

THE HUSBAND PULLED AND TUGGED AWAY TILL HE HAD NEARLY PULLED HIS WIFE'S HEAD OFF HER BODY.

She was just going to put it in the pan when her husband came in.

"Father, father!" cried the woman, "it's all over with our troubles and hard work now. I lent my brewing pan to a fine lady, and when she brought it back she promised we should have three wishes. And now you must help me to wish for something really good, for you're so clever at hitting upon the right thing—and it's all true, for just look at the sausage, which I got the moment I wished for it!"

"What do you mean, you silly old woman?" shouted the husband, who became angry. "Have you been wishing for such a paltry thing as a sausage, when you might have had anything you liked in the world? I wish that the sausage were sticking to your nose, since you haven't any better sense."

All at once the woman gave a cry, for sure enough there was the sausage sticking to her nose; and she began tearing and pulling away at it, but the more she pulled the firmer it seemed to stick. She was not able to get it off.

"Oh, dear! oh, dear!" sobbed the woman. "You don't seem to have any more sense than I, since you can wish me such ill luck. I only wanted something nice for you, and then——, oh, dear! oh, dear!" and the old woman went on crying and sobbing.

The husband tried, of course, to help his wife to get rid of the sausage; but for all he pulled and tugged away at it he did not succeed, and he was nearly pulling his wife's head off her body.

But they had one wish left, and what were they now to wish?

Yes, what were they to wish? They might, of course, wish for something very fine and grand; but what could they do with all the finery in the world, as long as the mistress of the house had a long sausage sticking to the end of her nose? She would never be able to show herself anywhere!

"You wish for something," said the woman in the midst of her crying.

"No, you wish," said the husband, who also began crying when he saw the state his wife was in, and saw the terrible sausage hanging down her face.

So he thought he would make the best use he could of the last wish, and said:

"I wish my wife was rid of that sausage."

And the next moment it was gone!

They both became so glad that they jumped up and danced round the room in great glee—for you must know that although a sausage may be ever so nice when you have it in your mouth, it is quite a different thing to having one sticking to your nose all your life.

THE OLD WOMAN AND THE TRAMP

There was once a tramp, who went plodding his way through a forest. The distance between the houses was so great that he had little hope of finding a shelter before the night set in. But all of a sudden he saw some lights between the trees. He then discovered a cottage, where there was a fire burning on the hearth. How nice it would be to roast one's self before that fire, and to get a bite of something, he thought; and so he dragged himself towards the cottage.

Just then an old woman came towards him.

"Good evening, and well met!" said the tramp.

"Good evening," said the woman. "Where do you come from?"

"South of the sun, and east of the moon," said the tramp; "and now I am on the way home again, for I have been all over the world with the exception of this parish," he said.

"You must be a great traveller, then," said the woman. "What may be your business here?"

"Oh, I want a shelter for the night," he said.

"I thought as much," said the woman; "but you may as well get away from here at once, for my husband is not at home, and my place is not an inn," she said.

"My good woman," said the tramp, "you must not be so cross and hard-hearted, for we are both human beings, and should help one another, it is written."

"Help one another?" said the woman, "help? Did you ever hear such a thing? Who'll help me, do you think? I haven't got a morsel in the house! No, you'll have to look for quarters elsewhere," she said.

But the tramp was like the rest of his kind; he did not consider himself beaten at the first rebuff. Although the old woman grumbled and complained as much as she could, he was just as persistent as ever, and went on begging and praying like a starved dog, until at last she gave in, and he got permission to lie on the floor for the night.

That was very kind, he thought, and he thanked her for it.

"Better on the floor without sleep, than suffer cold in the forest deep," he said; for he was a merry fellow, this tramp, and was always ready with a rhyme.

When he came into the room he could see that the woman was not so badly off as she had pretended; but she was a greedy and stingy woman of the worst sort, and was always complaining and grumbling.

He now made himself very agreeable, of course, and asked her in his most insinuating manner for something to eat.

"Where am I to get it from?" said the woman. "I haven't tasted a morsel myself the whole day."

But the tramp was a cunning fellow, he was.

"Poor old granny, you must be starving," he said. "Well, well, I suppose I shall have to ask you to have something with me, then."

"Have something with you!" said the woman. "You don't look as if you could ask any one to have anything! What have you got to offer one, I should like to know?"

"He who far and wide does roam sees many things not known at home; and he who many things has seen has wits about him and senses keen," said the tramp. "Better dead than lose one's head! Lend me a pot, grannie!"

The old woman now became very inquisitive, as you may guess, and so she let him have a pot.

He filled it with water and put it on the fire, and then he blew with all his might till the fire was burning fiercely all round it. Then he took a four-inch nail from his pocket, turned it three times in his hand and put it into the pot.

The woman stared with all her might.

"What's this going to be?" she asked.

"Nail broth," said the tramp, and began to stir the water with the porridge stick.

"Nail broth?" asked the woman.

"Yes, nail broth," said the tramp.

The old woman had seen and heard a good deal in her time, but that anybody could have made broth with a nail, well, she had never heard the like before.

"That's something for poor people to know," she said, "and I should like to learn how to make it."

"That which is not worth having, will always go a-begging," said the tramp.

But if she wanted to learn how to make it she had only to watch him, he said, and went on stirring the broth.

The old woman squatted on the ground, her hands clasping her knees, and her eyes following his hand as he stirred the broth.

"This generally makes good broth," he said; "but this time it will very likely be rather thin, for I have been making broth the whole week with the same nail. If one only had a handful of sifted oatmeal to put in, that would make it all right," he said. "But what one has to go without, it's no use thinking more about," and so he stirred the broth again.

"Well, I think I have a scrap of flour somewhere," said the old woman, and went out to fetch some, and it was both good and fine.

"WHAT'S THIS GOING TO BE?" ASKED THE WOMAN. "NAIL
BROTH," SAID THE TRAMP.

The tramp began putting the flour into the broth, and went on
stirring, while the woman sat staring now at him and then at the pot
until her eyes nearly burst their sockets.

"This broth would be good enough for company," he said, putting in
one handful of flour after another. "If I had only a bit of salted beef
and a few potatoes to put in, it would be fit for gentlefolks, however
particular they might be," he said. "But what one has to go without, it's
no use thinking more about."

When the old woman really began to think it over, she thought she had
some potatoes, and perhaps a bit of beef as well; and these she gave
the tramp, who went on stirring, while she sat and stared as hard as
ever.

"This will be grand enough for the best in the land," he said.

"Well, I never!" said the woman; "and just fancy—all with a nail!"

He was really a wonderful man, that tramp! He could do more than drink a sup and turn the tankard up, he could.

"If one had only a little barley and a drop of milk, we could ask the king himself to have some of it," he said; "for this is what he has every blessed evening—that I know, for I have been in service under the king's cook," he said.

"Dear me! Ask the king to have some! Well, I never!" exclaimed the woman, slapping her knees.

She was quite awestruck at the tramp and his grand connections.

"But what one has to go without, it's no use thinking more about," said the tramp.

And then she remembered she had a little barley; and as for milk, well, she wasn't quite out of that, she said, for her best cow had just calved. And then she went to fetch both the one and the other.

The tramp went on stirring, and the woman sat staring, one moment at him and the next at the pot.

Then all at once the tramp took out the nail.

"Now it's ready, and now we'll have a real good feast," he said. "But to this kind of soup the king and the queen always take a dram or two, and one sandwich at least. And then they always have a cloth on the table when they eat," he said. "But what one has to go without, it's no use thinking more about."

But by this time the old woman herself had begun to feel quite grand and fine, I can tell you; and if that was all that was wanted to make it just as the king had it, she thought it would be nice to have it just the same way for once, and play at being king and queen with the tramp. She went straight to a cupboard and brought out the brandy bottle, dram glasses, butter and cheese, smoked beef and veal, until at last the table looked as if it were decked out for company.

Never in her life had the old woman had such a grand feast, and never had she tasted such broth, and just fancy, made only with a nail!

31

She was in such a good and merry humour at having learnt such an economical way of making broth that she did not know how to make enough of the tramp who had taught her such a useful thing.

So they ate and drank, and drank and ate, until they became both tired and sleepy.

The tramp was now going to lie down on the floor. But that would never do, thought the old woman; no, that was impossible. "Such a grand person must have a bed to lie in," she said.

He did not need much pressing. "It's just like the sweet Christmas time," he said, "and a nicer woman I never came across. Ah, well! Happy are they who meet with such good people," said he; and he lay down on the bed and went asleep.

And next morning when he woke the first thing he got was coffee and a dram.

When he was going the old woman gave him a bright dollar piece.

"And thanks, many thanks, for what you have taught me," she said. "Now I shall live in comfort, since I have learnt how to make broth with a nail."

"Well, it isn't very difficult, if one only has something good to add to it," said the tramp as he went his way.

The woman stood at the door staring after him.

"Such people don't grow on every bush," she said.

WHAT SHALL BABY'S NAME BE?

There was once upon a time a worthy and well-to-do couple, who lived on the fat of the land, and had their house full of everything that was good and nice. But of children they had not many, for there was only one daughter in the house, and her they called Peggy, although she was christened Margaret, as you may guess.

Whatever the cause might be, whether the girl was ugly or whether there was anything else the matter with her, she grew up to be a big wench of full five and twenty years, and yet there was no suitor who would look at her.

"It's very strange," thought the father to himself; for all the lads in the parish knew, of course, that he had one of the finest farms, and many, many hundreds of dollars in money as well, and that he could give his daughter as a dowry both oxen and cows, goats and sheep, and that he would let his son-in-law take over the whole of the farm and keep the old folks till they died. He was never sparing with words on this subject. "Yes, they must be a silly, crack-brained lot when they don't avail themselves of such an opportunity, and get hold of one's only daughter," thought both the man and his wife. Peggy thought the same, although she did not say as much; but the lads seemed to keep away just as much as ever, for day after day passed, and year after year, but still no suitor came.

So one summer evening, as the man sat looking down the road and longing that a suitor might come, it happened that one of the best and smartest lads from one of the farms in the parish came strolling up the hill.

"Mother, mother!" cried the man. "I think he's coming at last! Come and have a look!"

His wife came running into the room and began staring out through the window.

"Well, what did I say?" she exclaimed. "If it isn't Peter South-farm! Sure enough it's he!"

She rushed out of the room again and began to bustle about and tidy her chamber, and called Peggy.

"Look out, wench! Now he's coming!"

"Whom do you mean, mother?"

"Why, your sweetheart, of course."

"Eh, you don't say so, mother!" cried Peggy, and became so pleased that she was quite beside herself.

And now they set to work to tidy and smarten themselves, and prepare something for the stranger who was coming up the road, for such a rare guest one could not expect every day.

In the meantime the suitor—for they had guessed quite rightly, a suitor it was—had entered the room, and greeted the man with a "good evening."

"Good evening," replied the man, and asked him to sit down. "One needs some rest, when one has walked up a steep hill like this," he said.

But the lad needed some pressing, it seemed.

He did not know if he would be welcome, he said; and so it was best that he should remain at the door till he had told his errand.

The man felt his heart leaping in his breast.

For many years he had longed for some one to come on such an errand, for he knew well what the lad was after.

"What errand might that be?" he asked.

"Well, it's rather an important matter," said the suitor.

The man called his wife, and she came in and greeted the lad.

"Excuse me—but may I ask," said the lad, "if there is a nice young girl here called Margaret?"

Yes, indeed there was—their only child, a big grown-up wench! And so clever with her hands—she could sew and stitch, spin and weave, both plain and striped and patterned—and she wasn't above taking off her gold ring and giving a hand at heavy work, if it was wanted. And then she was their only daughter, and was going to have the whole of the farm, the oxen and cows, the goats and sheep, the silver and gold, the clothes, the money and woven stuffs of all kinds as her dowry.

Both the man and his wife went on jabbering and chattering at the same time, and got so excited that it was with the greatest difficulty that the suitor was allowed to explain his errand.

She was just the girl he was looking out for, he said, and as he had no spokesman with him he would have to speak for himself, and tell them how he was off at home, and hear if they, who were her parents, would be satisfied with a son-in-law like him, he said.

"Well, that is quite possible," said the man. He himself was now so old and worn out and broken down with rheumatics that he wanted some one to take over the farm, so he could not very well refuse a good offer, he said. But one could not talk over such matters at the door; the lad must come inside, and partake of what his wife could offer.

"But this much I may say, at any rate," said the man, trying to put on a grand air, "that many have already spoken to me on the subject; but it is you, do you see, just you, that I have been waiting for," he said; "and you may reckon yourself lucky that you have not come too late. And, mother, you see, she agrees with everything I say—or, what do you think, mother?"

She had so much to attend to and look after, she said, but she was of the same mind as her husband. "And Peggy," said the man, "she is a good and obedient child. She does everything we tell her."

Peggy stood outside the door and kept it ajar, while she peeped through the opening, and would have said "yes" there and then, if it had only been proper. But she could not show herself too willing, either.

The man and the suitor now began to help themselves to the refreshments, and to talk about their farms and about the harvest, and about the number of cattle each of them could feed during the winter on their farms, and such things, while the wife was busy smartening up Peggy, whose head was so full of courtship and marriage that she was quite unfit to do anything for herself. But when she was dressed she looked very smart and shone like the sun, and then, as you may guess, she was to go in and see her suitor.

But she could not go in empty handed, and so her mother hit upon the idea—for women are always so artful—that Peggy should go down to the cellar for beer, and then come in to her suitor with the large silver cup in her hand.

While she was on her way down to the cellar she began thinking that when she was married it might easily happen that she, like others, would have a child; and then she went on thinking and pondering what she should call her first baby, for a name it must have, of course; but what should it be? Yes, what ought she to call it?

ON HER WAY DOWN TO THE CELLAR SHE BEGAN THINKING WHAT
SHE SHOULD CALL HER FIRST BABY.

But she could not make up her mind about it, although she thought
and pondered all she could, till at last she quite forgot both the cellar
and the beer, the suitor and the rest of the world. It was really not an
easy matter either, for she could not know whether it would be a boy

or a girl; but whatever it might be, the baby must have a name, and a really fine name, too, you must know.

But what should it be?

Yes, what should baby's name be?

While she stood there meditating her father and the suitor sat in the room partaking of the refreshments before them—smoked ham and cheese and other good things which the wife had in her cupboard.

One oatmeal cake after the other disappeared while they were waiting for the beer and the girl, and they began to think that the wolves must have got hold of her, since she did not come back.

"She is so shy and childish, that girl of mine," said the wife, "and I shouldn't wonder if she is afraid to come in. I shall have to fetch her, I suppose!"

And she hurried out to look for Peggy, whom she found standing outside the cellar-door, pondering and thinking.

"You are like Noah's raven, you are! How can a big wench like you stand there like that? I do believe you have lost your senses! Why don't you go in to your suitor?" said her mother. "What is it you are thinking about?"

"Oh, my dear mother," said Peggy, "I am just thinking what my first baby should be called. Can you tell me, mother?"

"Bless me, girl, if I can," said the woman; "but a name it must have, the little angel—and a fine name it must be. But what shall it be? Let me see."

And she too began thinking and remained standing there.

As neither his daughter nor his wife came back the man became uneasy.

"This is really too bad," he said, "that Peggy should make herself so precious. She is not generally so contrary, and I am sure that she'll say 'yes' just as willingly as we do," he said. "I suppose I must go myself and fetch her."

And so he limped out of the room as quickly as he could.

When he saw his wife and daughter standing outside the cellar-door he burst into a furious rage and shouted:

"I think you must have gone out of your minds, standing there like a pair of sundials, while you have got a suitor in the house! Just come in, will you?"

"Yes, yes," said the wife; "but I must tell you, we have been trying to settle a very ticklish business."

"Well, then, what might that be?" said the man.

"Why,—what shall Peggy's first baby be called?"

"Oh, is that it?" said the man, looking as tender and pleased as if he had the youngster on his arm. "So, that's it, is it?—Well, the baby must have a really fine name,—the little angel! But what shall we call it?— Yes, what shall we call it?"

He began to scratch his head and to think and ponder. He did not know either whether it would be a boy or a girl,—but no matter which it was, the baby must have a name, and what should it be called?—yes, what should they call it?

He couldn't make up his mind either, and so he remained standing there as well.

In the meantime the suitor had been sitting all by himself in the parlour, and was getting tired of waiting. So, as neither the maiden nor the old folks came back, he thought they must be doing it purposely, and had made up their minds to make a fool of him; whereupon he became furious, and took his hat and went.

When he came out into the farmyard he saw them all three standing outside the cellar-door.

The man caught sight of him first. "I must tell you, my lad," he said, "we have been standing here thinking over a very important matter,— and that is, what shall Peggy's first baby be called?"

"Good gracious!" said the suitor, "that'll surely bear thinking over, and you may have to think it over for a long time," he said, "for the baby will not be called after me! That's as certain as the sun rose this morning." And with that he lifted his hat and went down the hill.

The old man began to shout after him, but it was of no use. He went down the road and never came back again.

What happened afterwards I have not heard a word about; but if a suitor ever did call again, they would, no doubt, take care not to lose their heads over such useless speculations,—for we all know that there is a time for everything, and that we should strike while the iron is hot.

ST. PETER AND THE TWO WOMEN

In the days when St. Peter walked about on earth he came late one evening to a large farm, and asked for shelter for the night. The master was not at home, but his wife was sitting all alone; and although she was very rich and had an abundance of everything one could wish, she was niggardly beyond all belief. She could not give him shelter—was it likely she could?—and what should she give him to eat, and where should she put him? No, he would have to try somewhere else, she said; and, as there was no help for it, so he did.

When he had gone a little way he came to a small cottage, where there lived a poor widow, who struggled and toiled at spinning and weaving in order to scrape together a little food for herself and her children. St. Peter went into the parlour and told her his errand. The woman said, what was only too true, that she had little either of money or of food, but the little she had she would willingly share with him, since he had to go from house to house and beg for scraps of food—for she did not know it was St. Peter, nor did he say anything about it himself either.

So he got permission to stop there for the night, and he was quite welcome to what she could give him to eat. Early next morning he thanked her for her kindness and got ready to go.

"I have no money to pay you with," he said; "but what I can give I will give you. The first thing you do to-day you shall be doing all the day," he said.

The woman could not understand what he meant by this; but as soon as he was gone she took her yard-measure, for she had finished a piece of weaving and was going to take it off the loom in the evening, as she wanted to know how long it was.

She began to measure and to count, and she got to seventy, eighty, ninety and one hundred; but it was the most remarkable piece of cloth she had ever seen, for the more she measured the longer it became. The whole room became full of it, so that she had to go into the passage, but still there was no end to the piece.

"TWELVE AND TWENTY, THIRTEEN AND TWENTY, NINETEEN AND TWENTY," SAID
THE WIDOW. SHE HAD LOST COUNT, BUT STILL SHE KEPT ON
MEASURING.

The passage, too, became filled, so she had to go out on the grass. She measured and measured, but still the cloth grew longer, much longer than she could measure. She would not give in, but kept unceasingly at it the whole day. Towards evening the rich farmer's wife came past the cottage, and when she saw what the widow was doing she stopped all at once and wondered greatly at what she saw, for such a piece of weaving no human being had surely ever seen.

"What in all the world are you doing?" she asked.

"Twenty-three, twenty-four, twenty-five! Measuring a piece of weaving," said the widow. She was far on in the thirteenth hundred.

"Where in all the world have you got such a long piece from?" asked the woman.

"Twelve and twenty, thirteen and twenty, nineteen and twenty," said the widow—she had lost count, but still she kept on measuring. "Yes, you may well ask that," she said, and went on measuring. "A man came here last night and got a night's lodging, and when he left here this morning he said that the first thing I began with I should be doing the whole day; and now I have been measuring this cloth, which seems never to come to an end."

"Oh dear! oh dear! How stupid I was! How terribly stupid I was to let him go!" said the farmer's wife; "for he came to our place also, you must know. But, my dear, if he should ever come this way again and look in upon you you might send him to me, since you have been so lucky," she said.

Yes, that she would be glad to do, said the widow. She wished other people might be just as fortunate as she herself had been, although she had nothing to thank the farmer's wife for.

Of course, the widow could not use all the cloth herself, so she went to some of her neighbours to hire some oxen to cart it to town; and, just fancy, the cloth filled three cart-loads! Such a quantity of cloth had never been seen in one day in the market place; but she got rid of every yard for all that, and returned home with so much money that she had no longer any need to trouble about clothes and food.

But the rich farmer's wife went home and began to bustle about and get things ready, so that she should be able to treat the stranger in good style if he should come back to her; but she knew no more than the widow that the stranger was St. Peter.

She went about in great expectation, and dared scarcely go out of the room, so afraid was she that he should come in her absence and that she should miss him. She had bought a very fine piece of cloth and placed it on the loom, and the measure was lying on the top of it, so she was fully prepared for him; but day after day passed and week after week, and she grew angry and impatient because he was such a silly fellow not to have the sense to find his way there.

Late one evening there was a knock at the door.

41

The woman went out into the passage and pulled back the bolt. It was St. Peter, who asked for shelter for the night. Yes, that he should have, sure enough; and the woman curtseyed and behaved in a way that was quite ridiculous.

She then put the best she had on the table, so that he should be quite satisfied. In the morning he thanked her for her kindness and the good food, and prepared to go.

"YOU MIGHT AS WELL GIVE ME A PROMISE," SAID THE WOMAN, AND CURTSEYED.

"Just one word, my good man," said the woman; "when you got shelter at my neighbour's some time ago you gave her a promise, and you might as well give me one," she said, and curtseyed and made herself most agreeable and pleasant.

"What promise might that be?" asked St. Peter.

"Well, you said that whatever she began with she should be doing all the day," said the woman.

"Would you also like that?" said St. Peter.

"Should I like it? Why, my good man, of course, I should," said the woman. "I have the measure in my hand and the cloth handy."

"Well, I suppose I must do the same for you as for her then," said St. Peter; "so the first thing you do when I am gone you shall be doing the whole day. But, whatever you do, think it well over first," he said.

The woman curtseyed and thanked him, and was very happy and contented.

"Now I shall measure so much cloth that I shall have more than the poor body over yonder," she thought; and turned round and went back into the room.

Suddenly she remembered she ought to have drawn some water from the pump for her kettle, so that she could go on measuring the cloth without being disturbed. So she went to the pump and began to draw the water; but as this was the first thing she did after St. Peter was gone, there was no help for it—she must go on pumping water the whole day. The water came rushing out of the pump and ran all over the yard. It rose higher and higher as the hours crept by, and the woman began to shout and cry for help; but no one came to her assistance, and probably no one could have helped her either. When the sun was about to set the water had reached up to her chin. She was now quite exhausted, and all of a sudden she sank back into the water and was drowned. The yard measure and the cloth floated about on the water, and they may be floating there still for all I know.

THE OLD WOMAN AND THE FISH

There was once upon a time an old woman who lived in a miserable cottage on the brow of a hill overlooking the town. Her husband had been dead for many years, and her children were in service round about the parish, so she felt rather lonely and dreary in her cottage, and otherwise she was not particularly well off either.

43

But when it has been ordained that one shall live, one cannot think of one's funeral; and so one has to take the world as it is, and still be satisfied; and that was about all the old woman could console herself with. But that the road up which she had to carry the pails from the well should be so heavy; and that the axe should have such a blunt and rusty edge, so that it was only with the greatest difficulty that she could cut the little firewood she had; and that the stuff she was weaving was not sufficient;—all this grieved her greatly, and caused her to complain from time to time.

So one day, when she had pulled the bucket up from the well, she happened to find a small pike in the bucket, which did not at all displease her.

"Such fish does not come into my pot every day," she said; but now she could have a really grand dish, she thought. But the fish which she had got this time was no fool; it had the gift of speech, that it had.

"Let me go!" said the fish.

The old woman began to stare, you may be sure. Such a fish she had never before seen in this world.

"Are you so much better than other fish, then?" she said, "and too good to be eaten?"

"Wise is he who does not eat all he gets hold of," said the fish; "only let me go and you shall not remain without reward for your trouble."

"I like a fish in the bucket better than all those frisking about free and frolicsome in the lakes," said the old woman. "And what one can catch with one hand, one can also carry to one's mouth," she said.

"That may be," said the fish; "but if you do as I tell you, you shall have three wishes."

"Wish in one fist, and spit in the other, and you'll soon see which you will get filled first," said the woman. "Promises are well enough, but keeping them is better, and I sha'n't believe much in you till I have got you in the pot," she said.

"You should mind that tongue of yours," said the fish, "and listen to my words. Wish for three things, and then you'll see what will happen," he said.

44

Well, the old woman knew well enough what she wanted to wish, and there might not be so much danger in trying how far the fish would keep his word, she thought.

She then began thinking of the heavy hill up from the well.

"I would wish that the pails could go of themselves to the well and home again," she said.

"So they shall," said the fish.

Then she thought of the axe, and how blunt it was.

"I would wish that whatever I strike shall break right off," she said.

"So it shall," said the fish.

And then she remembered that the stuff she was weaving was not long enough.

"I would wish that whatever I pull shall become long," she said.

"That it shall," said the fish. "And now, let me down into the well again."

Yes, that she would, and all at once the pails began to shamble up the hill.

"Dear me, did you ever see anything like it?" The old woman became so glad and pleased that she slapped herself across the knees.

ALL AT ONCE THE PAILS BEGAN TO SHAMBLE UP THE HILL.

Crack, crack it sounded; and then both her legs fell off, and she was left sitting on the top of the lid over the well.

Now came a change. She began to cry and wail, and the tears started from her eyes, whereupon she began blowing her nose in her apron, and as she tugged at her nose it grew so long, so long that it was terrible to see.

That is what she got for her wishes! Well, there she sat, and there she no doubt still sits on the lid of the well. And if you want to know what it is to have a long nose, you had better go there and ask her, for she can tell you all about it, she can.

THE VALIANT CHANTICLEER

There was once upon a time a married couple who had no children, and they did not know what to do to get a child. The husband did not seem to mind so much, but the wife could not rest till she had a child. She must have one, whatever happened; and she went to doctors and wise men, and consulted all who knew a little more than other people, but to no avail. There was no one who could give her any advice.

So one evening an old woman came and asked for shelter for the night, which she got. But when women get together they always find something to talk about, and before long the wife had told the old woman all about herself and her affairs, and what a pity it was that she had no children.

"Is it no worse than that?" said the woman. "There's a way out of that! Look," she said, "here is an egg for you, and when you put it in your bosom and keep it nice and warm, you will soon have a little one, and a wonderful child it will be; such a child you have never seen," she said.

The wife thought this was strange, but there are so many strange things in this world that it was hardly worth while to wonder much about it. She took the egg and thanked the woman for her good advice, and said she would do as she was bid, and with this they parted.

She put the egg in her bosom and tended it well and carefully, and kept it as warm as she possibly could, and after a time a little cockerel flew out of it. The wife was not very pleased at this, you can understand, for she had not expected it would end in this way.

But as she had hatched him herself, she supposed he must be her child after all, such as he was. She looked after him and gathered food together for him, and cackled to him, and made herself as much like a hen as she could. And so he grew up and got both feathers and comb, and became so big, so big, that his equal had never been seen before.

When he was full-feathered he had to go out and find what he could, and he began to kick and scratch about in the dust heap, so that the rubbish was thrown up in the air so high that no one could see what became of it. But he wanted to try if he could do more than that, and so he strutted out into the corn-field, where the master of the house was toiling away and ploughing with the one ox he possessed. But he got on very slowly, so the cock thought he ought to help him. So he was yoked to the plough; and then things took a different turn, for now they went at such a speed that the master had to run as fast as he could, and in a little while the cock had ploughed the whole field. He now thought he was a full-grown fellow, and that he could get married; but not to a little farm-yard hen, that would never do for him. No, he must look higher, and so he flapped his wings and crowed.

"The king's daughter shall be mine!" and he wanted to set out for the king's palace.

But he must have a suitable conveyance for the bride, he thought, even if he had to drag it himself; and as there was nothing else to be found, he took the big soup-ladle. The wife cried and cackled after him, but out into the world he must go, and away he went.

All at once he met a fox.

"Where are you going?" asked the fox.

"To the king's palace," crowed the cock.

"May I come with you?" said the fox.

"Sit up behind," cried the cock; and the fox took a seat in the ladle, and away they went.

Then he met a wolf.

"Where are you going?" asked the wolf.

"To the king's palace," crowed the cock.

"May I come with you?" said the wolf.

"Sit up behind," cried the cock; and then the wolf seated himself in the ladle, and away they went.

Then the cock met a bear.

"Where are you going?" asked the bear.

"To the king's palace," crowed the cock.

"May I come with you?" said the bear.

"Sit up behind," cried the cock; and then the bear took a seat in the ladle, and away they went.

All at once they came to a lake.

"Where are you going?" asked the lake.

"To the king's palace," crowed the cock.

"May I come with you?" said the lake.

"Sit up behind," cried the cock; and then the lake began to heave, so that the one billow after the other washed up into the ladle, and soon the whole lake was in it. The cock's companions got a little wet about the feet, but there was no help for that. The cock set off with them, and so they came to the king's palace. The cock now flew up on the roof of the palace and crowed:

"The king's daughter shall be mine!"

The king heard this.

"That's a strange cock!" he thought. And then he gave orders that his men should catch him, and all of them began to run after the cock and call him. But when they got so near to him that they could almost catch him, he flew up on the roof again, and then he crowed:

"The king's daughter shall be mine!"

It was all in vain, they could not catch him.

"I suppose you must have her, then," said the king, with a laugh; and then the cock allowed himself to be caught at once.

But as soon as the king had got him he was sorry for what he had promised, for a king's word is a king's word; but a better son-in-law he might surely have got—he who had such a fair and beautiful daughter, and his only daughter into the bargain. But how should he get rid of him?

"If I let him into the goose-pen, the geese are sure to finish him off," he thought; and so he let the cock in among the geese. They began to pinch and peck at him with their beaks and to pluck his feathers out, but just then he crowed for the fox:

"Cock-a-doodle-do! Foxie, come and help!"

And the fox came sneaking along, and he was not slow in getting in among the geese, and there he ravaged about in such a way that they were all dead in less than no time.

49

The cock then flew up on the roof, and crowed:

"The king's daughter shall be mine!"

"Such a dreadful cock I have never set eyes on!" thought the king. "Now he has killed all my geese! How shall I get rid of him? What if I let him in among my cattle? They'll be sure to finish him," he thought, and so he let him into the cow-shed. The king had a large herd of cattle, and they seized the cock with their horns and tossed him about between them like a ball.

But the cock flew up on top of the bull and crowed for the wolf:

"Cock-a-doodle-do! Wolfie, come and help!"

The wolf was not long in coming, and he had such a feast that there wasn't a single beast left alive.

The cock flew up on the roof again, and then he crowed:

"The king's daughter shall be mine!"

"Has any one seen the like of that cock?" said the king. "Now he has finished all my geese and all my cattle. How shall I get rid of him? What if I let him in among the horses? They'll be sure to finish him," he thought; and so he let the cock into the stable.

The king had a lot of horses, and they began to rear and kick with all their might, so that the cock was knocked about from one to the other like a wheel rolling down the street, and he soon got tired of that kind of knocking about. So he crowed for the bear.

"Cock-a-doodle-do! Bruin, come and help!"

And the bear was not long in coming, and he began to strike and tear, till there was not one of the king's horses left.

The cock then flew up on the roof again, and crowed:

"The king's daughter shall be mine!"

"That's the worst cock I ever came across," said the king. "First he kills all my geese and all my cattle, and now he has finished my horses as well. I shall be quite ruined. But now I'll put him on the spit and roast him and eat him myself, and it'll be a wonder if I don't get rid of him then." That was what must be done; and so they took the cock and put him on the spit, and the kitchenmaids made such a big fire, that it fizzled all round him. But the cock crowed for the lake.

"Cock-a-doodle-do! Lakey, come and help!"

And the lake came rolling in and put out the fire. But it was only just in the nick of time,—for the cock was half roasted. But as they could not get him done any better, he would have to do as he was; and so they carried him up on a silver dish and placed him on the table. The king was so angry that he swallowed him in one gulp.

"Now I suppose I'm rid of him," he thought.

But had anybody heard the like?

As soon as the cock got into the king's stomach he began to revive again and to crow:

"The king's daughter shall be mine!" And he tumbled about so terribly down there that the king could not keep him down, and so had to vomit him. But no sooner had the cock recovered than he began to flap his wings, and he flew up and perched on the top of the king's crown, and there he crowed:

"The king's daughter shall be mine!"

The king was in despair; he did not know what to do, and flung his crown away.

THE COCK TRIED TO COMFORT THE PRINCESS AS BEST HE
COULD, AND SWEPT THE TABLE WITH HIS WINGS.

"Well, you had better take her then, you bird of ill-omen, and half the
kingdom as well; only leave me in peace!" he cried.

The cock was now to have the princess. She cried and wept bitterly, for
you can easily understand she did not want such a bridegroom. She was
not a hen, and did not want to become one.

But all her crying and her wailings were of no avail, she would have to
marry the cock and be satisfied with him. He tried to comfort her as
best he could, and swept the table with his wings, and breasted and

plumed himself in a cock's very best manner; but she went on crying and weeping, and as he was not able to console her, he at last asked her to wring his neck. No, that she would not do, for life may be dear, even to a cock, she thought. But he begged and prayed so hard that at last she did it, and the next moment a prince stood before her, and he was so fine and handsome as to beggar all description; and yet he was the cock! There was soon an end to the crying and wailing, and things took another turn, for both the princess and the king were so happy that no one can believe how happy they were.

To the wedding came people from all parts of the country, and the man and his wife were there as well. The fox and the wolf and the bear waited at the table, and the lake washed up the dishes, and altogether it was the grandest wedding I have ever been to in all my days.

TWIGMUNTUS, COWBELLIANTUS, PERCHNOSIUS

Once upon a time there was a king who was so very learned that no parson in the whole world could surpass him; in fact, he was so learned that ordinary folks could hardly understand what he said, nor could he understand them either. But in order to have some one to talk with he procured seven wise professors, who were not quite so learned as himself, but who were just able to interpret his learned sayings, so that people could apprehend them, and who could twist and turn about the talk of ordinary folk so that it became sufficiently learned and complicated for the king to understand it.

The king had no son, but he had a daughter, and in order that she should be happily married, and the country governed according to the fundamental principles of his learning, he issued an edict that he who was so learned as to put the king and his professors to silence should have his daughter and half the kingdom there and then. But any one who attempted the task and did not succeed, should lose his head for having dared to exchange words with the king.

That was no joke; but the princess was so fair and beautiful that it was no joke to gaze at her either. And the king did not keep her caged up, for any one who wished could see her.

There came princes and counts and barons and parsons and doctors, and learned persons from all quarters of the world; and no sooner did they see the princess than they one and all wanted to try their luck. But, however learned they were, their learning never proved sufficient, and every one of them lost his head.

Over in a corner of the kingdom there lived a farmer, who had a son. This lad was not stupid; he was quick of apprehension and sharp witted, and he was not afraid of any thing.

When the king's edict came to this out-of-the-way place, and the parson had read it from the pulpit, the lad wanted to try his luck. "He who nothing risks, nothing wins," thought the lad; and so he went to the parson and told him that if he would give him lessons in the evenings, he would work for the parson in the daytime, but he wanted to become so learned that he could try a bout with the king and his professors.

"Whoever means to compete with them must be able to do something more than munch bread," said the parson.

"That may be," said the lad; "but I'll try my luck."

The parson thought, of course, that he was mad; but when he could get such a clever hand to work for him only for his keep, he thought he could not very well say no; and so the lad got what he wanted.

He worked for the parson in the daytime, and the parson read with him in the evening; and in this way they went on for some time, but at last the lad grew tired of his books.

"I am not going to sit here and read and grind away, and lose what few wits I have," he said; "and it won't be of much help either, for if you are lucky things will come right of themselves, and if you are not lucky you'll never make a silk purse out of a sow's ear."

And with this he pitched the books on the shelf and went his way.

All at once he came to a large forest, where the trees and the bushes were so thick that it was with difficulty he could get along. While he was thus pushing his way through, he began wondering what he should say when he came to the king's palace, and how best he could make use of the learning he had picked up from the parson. All of a sudden the twig of a tree struck him across his mouth, so that his teeth rattled.

"That is Twigmuntus," he said.

A little while after he came to a meadow, where a cow was standing bellowing so furiously that it almost deafened him.

"That is Cowbelliantus," he said.

He then came to a river; but as there was neither bridge nor planks across it, he had to put his clothes on his head and swim across.

While he was swimming a perch came and bit him on the nose.

"That is Perchnosius," he said.

At last he came to the king's palace, where things did not look at all pleasant, for there were men's heads stuck on long stakes round about, and they grinned so horribly that they were enough to frighten any one out of his wits. But the lad was not easily frightened.

"God's peace!" he said, and raised his cap. "There you stick and grin at me; but who knows if I may not be keeping you company before the day is over, and be grinning with you at others? But if I happen to be alive, you shall not stick there any longer gaping at people," he said.

So he went up to the palace and knocked at the gate.

The guard came out and asked what he wanted.

"I have come to try my luck with the princess," said the lad.

"You?" said the guard, "well, you're a likely one, you are! Have you lost your senses? There have been princes and counts and barons and parsons and doctors and learned persons here, and all of them have had to pay with their heads for that pleasure; and yet you think you'll succeed!" he said.

"I should say it is no concern of yours," said the lad; "just open the gate, and you'll see one who's not afraid of anything."

But the guard would not let him in.

"Do as I tell you," said the lad, "or there'll be a fine to-do!"

But the guard would not.

The lad then seized him by the collar and flung him against the wall, so that it creaked; and then he walked straight in to the king, who sat in his parlour with all his seven professors about him. Their faces were long and thin, and they looked like puny sickly persons about to die. They were sitting with their heads on one side meditating and staring at the floor.

Then one of them, who looked up, asked the lad in ordinary language: "Who are you?"

"A suitor," said the lad.

"Do you want to try for the princess's hand?"

"Well, that's about it!" said the lad.

"Have you lost your wits? There have been princes and counts and barons and parsons and doctors and learned persons here, and all of them have gone headless away; so you had better turn about and get away while your head is on your shoulders," he said.

"Don't trouble yourself on that account, but rather think of the head on your own shoulders," said the lad. "You look after yours, and I'll take care of mine! So just begin, and let me hear how much wit you have got, for I don't think you look so very clever," he said.

The first professor then began a long harangue of gibberish; and when he had finished the second went on; and then the third; and in this way they continued till at length it was the turn of the seventh. The lad did not understand a single word of it all, but he didn't lose courage for all that. He only nodded his approval to all of it.

When the last had finished his harangue he asked:

"Can you reply to that?"

"That's easy enough," said the lad. "Why, when I was in my cradle and in my go-cart I could twist my mouth about and prate and jabber like you," he said. "But since you are so terribly learned, I'll put a question to you, and that shall not be a long one:

"Twigmuntus, Cowbelliantus, Perchnosius? Can you give me an answer to that?"

And now you should have seen how they stretched their necks and strained their ears. They put on their spectacles and began to look into their books and turn over the leaves.

But while they were searching and meditating, the lad put his hands in his trouser pockets, and looked so frank and fearless that they could not help admiring him, and wondering that one who was so young could be so learned and yet look just like other people.

"Well, how are you getting on?" said the lad. "Cannot all your learning help you to open your mouths, so that I can have an answer to my question?" he said.

Then they began to ponder and meditate, and then they glanced at the ceiling, and then they stared at the walls, and then they fixed their eyes upon the floor. But they could not give him any answer, nor could the king himself, although he was much more learned than all the others together. They had to give it up, and the lad got the princess and half the kingdom. This he ruled in his own way, and if it did not fare better, it did not fare worse for him than for the king with all his fundamental principles.

THE LAD AND THE FOX

There was once upon a time a little lad, who was on his way to church, and when he came to a clearing in the forest he caught sight of a fox, who was lying on the top of a big stone fast asleep, so that the fox did not know the lad had seen him.

"If I kill that fox," said the lad, taking a heavy stone in his fist, "and sell the skin, I shall get money for it, and with that money I shall buy some rye, and that rye I shall sow in father's cornfield at home. When the people who are on their way to church pass by my field of rye they'll say: 'Oh, what splendid rye that lad has got!' Then I shall say to them: 'I say, keep away from my rye!' But they won't heed me. Then I shall shout to them: 'I say, keep away from my rye!' But still they won't take any notice of me. Then I shall scream with all my might: 'Keep away from my rye!' and then they'll listen to me."

But the lad screamed so loudly that the fox woke up and made off at once for the forest, so that the lad did not even get as much as a handful of his hair.

No; it's best always to take what you can reach, for of undone deeds you should never screech, as the saying goes.

OLD NICK AND THE GIRL

There was once a girl who was so mad about dancing that she nearly went out of her mind whenever she heard a fiddle strike up.

She was a very clever dancer, and a smarter girl to whirl round in a dance or kick her heels was not easily to be found, although she only had shoes made of birch-bark, and knitted leggings on her feet. She swept past at such a rate that the air whistled round her like a humming top. She might have whirled round still more quickly and lightly, of course, if she had had leather shoes. But how was she to get them, when she had no money to pay for them? For she was very poor, this girl, and could ill afford them.

So one day, when the fair was being held at Amberg Heath, whom should she meet but Old Nick! He was going to see the fun of the fair, as you may guess, for all sorts of tramps and vagabonds and watch-dealers and rogues go there; and where such gentry are to be found, others of the same feather are sure to flock together.

"What are you thinking about?" asked Old Nick, who knew well enough how matters stood.

"I am wondering how I shall be able to get a pair of leather shoes to dance in," said the girl; "for I haven't any money to pay for them," she said.

"Is that all? We'll soon get over that," said Old Nick, and produced a pair of leather shoes, which he showed her. "Do you like these?" he asked.

The girl stood staring at the shoes. She could never have believed that there were such fine, splendid shoes, for they were not common ones sewn with pitched thread, but real German shoes with welted soles, and looked as French as one could wish.

"Is there a spring in them as well?" she asked.

"Yes, that you may be sure of," said Old Nick. "Do you want them?"

Yes, that she did; there could be no doubt about that, and so they began bargaining and higgling about the payment, till at last they came to terms. She was to have the shoes for a whole year for nothing, if only she would dance in his interest, and afterwards she should belong to him.

She did not exactly make a good bargain, but Old Nick is not a person one can bargain with. But there was to be such a spring in them that no human being would be able to swing round quicker in a dance or kick higher than she did; and if they did not satisfy her, he would take them back for nothing, and she should be free.

With this they parted.

And now the girl seemed to wake up thoroughly. She thought of nothing else but going to dances, wherever they might be, night after night. Well, she danced and danced, and before she knew it the year came to an end, and Old Nick came and asked for his due.

"They were a rubbishy pair of shoes you gave me," said the girl; "there was no spring at all in them," she said.

"Wasn't there any spring in the shoes? That's very strange," said Old Nick.

"No, there wasn't!" said the girl. "Why, my bark shoes are far better, and I can get on much faster in them than in these wretched things."

"You twist about as if you were dancing," said Old Nick; "but now I think you will have to dance away with me after all."

"Well, if you don't believe my words, I suppose you'll believe your eyes," she said. "Put on these grand shoes of yours, and try them yourself," she said, "and I'll put on my bark shoes, and then we'll have a race, so that you can see what they are good for," she said.

Well, that was reasonable enough, he thought, and, no doubt, he felt there was very little danger in trying it. So they agreed to race to the end of Lake Fryken and back, one on each side of the lake, which, as you know, is a very long one indeed. If she came in first she was to be free, but if she came in last she was to belong to him.

But the girl had to run home first of all, for she had a roll of cloth for the parson, which she must deliver before she tried her speed with Old Nick. Very well, that she might, for he went in fear of the parson; but the race should take place on the third day afterwards.

Now, as bad luck would have it for Old Nick, it so happened that the girl had a sister, who was so like her that it was impossible to know one from the other, for they were twins, the two girls.

But the sister was not mad about dancing, so Old Nick had not got scent of her. The girl now asked her sister to place herself at Frykstad, the south end of the lake, and she herself took up her position at Fryksend, the north end of it.

She had the bark shoes on, and Old Nick the leather ones; and so they set off, each on their side of the lake. The girl did not run very far, for she knew well enough how little running she need do; but Old Nick set off at full speed, much faster than one can ride on the railway.

But when he came to Frykstad he found the girl already there; and when he came back to Fryksend there she was too.

"Well, you see now?" said the girl.

OLD NICK SET OFF AT A TERRIBLE SPEED; IT WAS JUST LIKE
A REGULAR NORTH-WESTER RUSHING PAST.

"Of course I see," said Old Nick, but he was not the man to give in at once. "One time is no time, that you know," he said.

"Well, let's have another try," said the girl.

Yes, that he would, for the soles of his shoes were almost worn out, and then he knew what state the bark shoes would be in.

They set off for the second time, and Old Nick ran so fast that the air whistled round the corners of the houses in Sanne and Emtervik parishes; but when he came to Frykstad, the girl was already there, and when he got back to Fryksend, she was there before him this time also.

"Can you see now who comes in first?" she said.

"Yes, of course I can," said Old Nick, and began to dry the perspiration off his face, thinking all the time what a wonderful runner that girl must be. "But you know," he said, "twice is hardly half a time! It's the third time that counts."

"Let's have another try, then," said the girl.

Yes, that he would, for Old Nick is very sly, you know, for when the leather shoes were so torn to pieces that his feet were bleeding, he knew well enough what state the bark shoes would be in.

And so they set off again. Old Nick went at a terrible speed; it was just like a regular north-wester rushing past, for now he was furious. He rushed onwards, so that the roofs were swept away and the fences creaked and groaned all the way through Sonne and Emtervik parishes. But when he got to Frykstad the girl was there, and when he got back to Fryksend then she was there too.

OLD NICK HAD NOW TO ACKNOWLEDGE HIMSELF BEATEN.

His feet were now in such a plight that the flesh hung in pieces from them, and he was so out of breath, and groaned so hard, that the sound echoed in the mountains. The girl almost pitied the old creature, disgusting as he was.

"Do you see, now," she said, "that there's a better spring in my bark shoes than in your leather ones? There's nothing left of yours, while mine will hold out for another run, if you would like to try," she said.

No, Old Nick had now to acknowledge himself beaten, and so she was free.

"I've never seen the like of such a woman," he said; "but if you go on dancing and jumping about like that all your days we are sure to meet once more," he said.

"Oh, no!" said the girl. And since then she has never danced again, for it is not every time that you can succeed in getting away from Old Nick.

THE STONE STATUE

There were once two men who were walking across a churchyard—and there was nothing remarkable about that; but when one of them lifted his cap, as one should do in such a place, and said: "God's peace to all who rest here!" then the other said: "They lie as they have made their bed, and they get what they deserve!" It was very wicked to talk in that way; and no sooner had he spoken these words than he was changed into a stone statue, and thus he stood for many, many years. The one parson after the other came and prayed and chanted over him, but no one was able to exorcise the soul out of the petrified body.

It so happened that a new parson came to the parish, and he was much more learned than all the others. He was a model parson in every respect; but he was somewhat hasty, and his wife was not one to be trifled with either. When he saw the stone statue and heard why it stood there, he wanted also to try to get its soul to rest in peace. He had the statue carried into his study, so that he could pray over it every day, both in the morning and in the evening and at all hours of the day, which he did. But the first time he read the evening prayers and came to the words: "God banish everything that is evil from this house!" he heard something like a titter over in the corner where the statue stood, but he could not make out from whom it proceeded. Next evening when he came to these words the same thing happened, but he became none the wiser this time either.

The third evening he again heard the same tittering; but this time he kept a better watch, and then he discovered it was the statue over in the corner that had tittered.

"Can you laugh?" said the parson. "If so, I suppose you can tell me what you are laughing at?"

Yes, that the statue could.

"You see, reverend father," said the statue, "you are wonderfully learned in all sorts of divine teachings, and you live, no doubt, according to what you teach; but you quarrel a little too much with your wife, and therefore all the house swarms with little imps during the day. When you read the evening prayers and come to the words: 'God banish every thing that is evil from this house!' they have to take themselves off; and there is one among them, a little fellow who limps and who tosses his body about in such a funny way when he trudges along, that one cannot help laughing at him. But although they take to flight when you read the prayers, it is not long before they are back again; and as soon as you and your wife begin to quarrel this limping little rascal comes hobbling in, and then all the other little devils come prowling after him, one after the other."

Those words made the parson's heart ache, for when stones begin to talk it is well to listen.

And this he did. He became more forbearing to his wife, and as she herself was not particularly fond of these crawling little things, whom she could not see, but who swarmed around her, she also tried, as well as she could, to control her temper. And as both of them were now more friendly to one another and more inclined to give way to each other, they began little by little to agree and to get on well together. And after a while the statue was not heard to say anything either; and some little time afterwards the parson asked it if it now saw any signs of the little hobbling imp and his companions.

"Well, I have seen him holding the door ajar and peeping in, but he has not ventured across the threshold," said the statue; "but now I think he has become tired of it, for he has not been here for many days, and now I only see God's angels around you."

The parson rejoiced at hearing these words, and thanked God for having put an end to all their dissensions.

WHEN HE READ THE EVENING PRAYERS HE HEARD SOMETHING
LIKE A TITTER OVER IN THE CORNER.

"But how is it with yourself now?" he asked the statue.

"Well, I shall also find peace now," said the statue; "for now I have done a good deed, and I am only waiting for the last prayer."

And it was not long before it came. The parson read the best prayer he knew, and when he had finished the statue became flesh and blood again, but he drew his last breath at the same moment. The parson put him in a coffin and gave him a respectable burial, and in this way they both benefited.

THE ARTFUL LAD

There were once two farmers whose farms lay side by side in the same parish. Their land was of the same size and equally taxed, so that by rights both the farmers ought to have been equally well off. But they were not; for the one was rich, and the other was only just able to keep body and soul together. You may think this was strange, since the one was just as industrious as the other; but it was not so very strange after all, for the rich farmer had a servant lad to help him—and a very clever lad he was, while the other had to do all the work himself, and did not even get any help from his wife, for she suffered so much from internal complaints, she said, that she was unable to do any work in the fields. Nor did she do much indoor work, at which she had to sit quiet; but spin and wind yarn, and run about from one room to the other, that she could do. And as for her complaint, it could not be as bad as she pretended, for she did not look either ill or ailing. No, on the contrary she was stout and trim, and red in the face like a peony; and although she was short and stout, she was broad both across her shoulders and hips, so that no one could find anything amiss with her. But she was one of those who will steal away from work and idle her time away; and that was about all that ailed her. And she had the habit of hiding away all that her husband brought home with him in his ox-cart, and so you may guess things could not last very long. The farmer was greatly to be pitied, although no one thought of pitying him; for if only he had given his wife a beating now and then it would have been all the better for him. But this he neglected to do, and so he had to suffer for it; there was no help for it.

So one Sunday morning, when his wife was out gallivanting about, as was her custom early and late, the farmer was sitting alone in his parlour, and a strange lad happened to come in.

"Good evening, master!" said the lad.

"Good evening!" said the farmer.

"Do you want a servant lad, master?"

"A servant lad? God help me," said the farmer, "how can I afford that? I can scarcely manage to keep and feed myself, worse luck!"

"Is that so?" said the lad. "But that's just the reason why you want some one to help you."

"You talk as if you hadn't any sense," said the farmer. "If two mouths can empty a dish, does one get any the more when a hungry body stands by staring at one? And if the stuff for one's breeches is not enough for two legs, is it likely to be sufficient for four?"

"Of course," said the lad, "if only you use your wits; for if you use them, you need not be without either bread or breeches, that's certain, and that you may depend upon. And I'll take care to manage things, and to stretch the stuff for the breeches, so that it will be sufficient both for you and for me—that's to say, if the missis does not wear the breeches," he said.

"You have a bold tongue, my lad," said the farmer; "but it's one thing to boast and brag, and another to work and drag; and braggarts are generally the greatest sluggards,—have you heard that?"

"Yes, I have. I have heard that and a good deal more," said the lad. "But that's neither here nor there. I like this place, and here I'll remain, and as for wages we are sure to agree about them. I don't want to take anything from you till I've earned it."

"How you do talk!" said the farmer. "You talk and you talk till my ears tingle, but that's an easy matter, and big words often lead to a big fall; but if you can manage to get along on scanty fare, there will not be much risk about it," he said.

"Well, you take the risk, master, and you'll not regret it," said the lad. "For I am the lad who's not afraid of anything."

The farmer began to scratch his head. He liked the lad, for you must know he was a big, strong fellow, and if he were only half as strong as he looked, he would still be one of the strongest in the parish. But it would require more than water-gruel to feed such a fellow properly. What should he feed him on? And his wife was not at home either. What would she say when she found she had such a big eater in the house? What should they give him to eat?

"Well," said the boy, who began to be impatient, "what's your answer?"

"Well, that's just what I am thinking about," said the farmer.

"But that's of little good to me," said the lad. "Listen to me! Don't sit pondering and pondering, or it'll fare with you as with the parson who walked up and down the vestry pondering upon his first sermon till all the people had left the church. No, that won't do! Quick thoughts belong to a quick head, so don't make yourself more stupid than you are! Here's my hand!" he said.

Well, the farmer had to hold out his hand too, which the lad squeezed so hard that the farmer yelled; and that was the whole contract. But what was done was done; and the wife might think what she liked, for the lad went to his work at once, he did.

All at once the wife came rushing in.

"Good evening! Glad to see you back!" said the farmer.

"Good evening, husband!" said the wife. "How have you been amusing yourself while I have been out?" she said, in an insinuating voice and with a mild look in her eyes.

"Well, I've taken a servant lad!" said the farmer.

"Servant lad?" said the wife. "Have you gone clean out of your senses? Taken a servant lad, you say?"

"Yes, just so!" said the farmer.

"Bless me!" said the woman, clasping her hands in surprise. "Has any one ever heard the like? What are we going to pay him and feed him with, I should like to know?"

"His wages will be my affair, and the feeding yours," said the farmer.

"I pity him, poor fellow," said the wife.

"You needn't pity me at all," said the lad, "for I'm the sort of lad that isn't afraid. How do you do, mother? We shall be the best of friends and get on well together," he said.

The wife had to shake hands with him; and when she looked a little closer at him, she saw he was a fine fellow, who had his wits about him. 'That fellow is not to be trifled with,' she thought, but she did not say a word. And the lad did not speak a word either. He only stared at her, as she sat by the hearth, looking as fat and round in the face as a pancake; and then he looked at the farmer and saw how thin and gaunt and sallow he was. "What a fiend of a woman! She must eat something better than water-gruel," thought the lad.

On the following Monday the farmer and the lad set out early in the morning to the forest to cut trees for hurdles. When they got there, the

68

lad remembered that he had forgotten his axe. So he had to run home again. He went into the parlour and found that his mistress was out, but there was a cloth on the table, and he could see she had not put it there to be bleached by the sun, for there was bread and butter and cheese and even brandy on the table. Had any one ever seen such a woman? That was quite another sort of breakfast to the water-gruel and bread-crumbs she gave her husband.

"There's something wrong in this house," he thought, "but take your time and you'll see." And so he crept into the settle-bed, and shut down the lid over him, and then he cut a little peep-hole in the side of the bed.

All at once the woman came hurrying in, bringing her neighbour with her. She asked him to sit down and make himself at home, which he lost no time in doing.

"I heard you were going to the forest to-day, and so I thought you would like a tit-bit and a dram," she said, and made herself as caressing and pleasant as a westerly breeze on a midsummer night. Her guest needed no persuasion, and it wasn't necessary to ask him twice. He ate and drank and helped himself to one dram after another. The woman was not backward either. She drank a glass with him, and chattered away and made herself as pleasant as she could. In the meantime the lad lay inside the settle-bed, chewing a bit of straw and peeping through the hole and listening all the while.

When the neighbour had finished his breakfast, he had eaten so much that he had to loosen the strap of his leathern apron, and then he got ready to go.

"Just wait a bit," said the woman. "Where will you be working to-day?"

"I shall be in the forest close to where your people are cutting," he said.

"Will you be alone?" she asked.

Yes, that he would, he said, for his lad had gone to the mill.

"If you will mark the trees and drop branches in the path, I'll come and bring you some dinner," she said.

"Thank you," said the neighbour as he went out; and so the woman went into the kitchen.

Then the lad jumped out of the settle-bed and made his way back to the forest.

Well, the neighbour did as the woman had told him, but as he went through the forest and lopped off branches, the lad, who was following behind, picked them up and marked the path leading to the place where his master was working.

He thought he had managed things very well.

In the meantime his master had been hewing away till the splinters flew, and swore because the lad did not come back.

"How stupid I was! What did I want with a lazy-bones like that," he thought. "He can boast and brag, but he is not so smart on his legs as with his tongue, that I can see; and if he goes on like this the first day, what will the end be?"

Just then the lad came back. He had lost his way in the forest, he said, and he had had to turn his jacket three times [1] before he got on the right path.

"With the lazy ox the Huldre drives best," the farmer said; "and I should like to know whether you belong to her people or mine," he said, and was very angry.

"Bide your time, and you'll see," said the lad, and set to work with a will.

He cut away till the forest thundered and rang with his blows, so that in a short time he had felled more trees than the farmer.

"Will that do?" he said.

"It will," said the farmer.

The lad then put down the axe and began to look round.

"What are you staring after?" said the farmer.

"I can see by the sun that it's dinner-time," said the lad; "and I am looking for my mistress, for I think it's about time that she ought to be here with our dinner."

"Is that what you are staring after?" said the farmer. "If so, you'll be staring till your eyes start out of your head, for mother said she hadn't got anything for us; so we shall have to cut and hew as long as we are able, and even when we get home I don't think we shall be able to scrape much together."

"Bless me!" said the lad, "we mustn't think it'll be as bad as that! Oh no, the mistress will be coming, you'll see, and you may depend she'll give us a good meal."

"Well, believe it if you like," said the farmer. "But if you can manage with that sort of food till this evening you'll not be difficult to keep," he said.

And with this he tightened the leather apron round his waist and began to fell trees again.

"Look there, master!" said the lad.

The farmer did stare, you may guess, for he saw his wife stealing along between the bushes with a big bag of food on her arm.

She did not take her eyes off the ground, as she was looking for the branches, and she didn't know where she was till she was close up to her husband.

"Well, mother!" said the farmer.

His wife gave a start.

"Good gracious, is that you?" she said.

"Of course it's me," said the farmer, and laughed. "Surely you ought to know that when you come here with the dinner. But sit down, and let me see what you have been able to scrape together for us."

He then took the bag and began to see what she had brought.

There was butter and cheese and there was pease pudding. "Ey, hey!" said the farmer, smacking his lips. And there was sweet cheese and cheese cakes, too.

"I can hardly believe my eyes! Why, this'll be quite a grand feast, mother!" said he. He then found a little bottle. What could there be in that bottle? He took out the cork. It was brandy. He became so pleased that he gave his wife a dig in the ribs, so that she went sprawling along the ground.

"I say, mother," he cried, "where have you got all these good things from? You haven't stolen them, I hope?"

"Oh, they are some trifles I have been saving up," she said, "and I thought they would just do to-day, since it is the first dinner we give our new lad," she said; but most likely she wished both the lad and her husband as far away as possible, and a little bit farther, as you may guess, for it was their neighbour she was looking for, and he, poor fellow, would not even be able to get a sniff of the good things.

But she was a cunning woman, and that kind of woman always finds a way out of difficulties.

"I say, husband," she said, "our neighbour is in the forest too to-day, and we have never offered him any hospitality. Won't you ask him to come here and have something?"

The farmer was not particularly anxious to get any help, for there was not overmuch of food in the bag, and he and the lad could easily manage what there was, he thought; but he was not mean, nor did he want to go against his wife either.

"Run and ask our neighbour, then," he said to the lad; and off went the lad, but first he took a large piece of cheese with him. He would eat that on the way, he said, for the water-gruel and bread-crumbs which he had had for breakfast had disappeared long ago, so he was very hungry, he said. But he broke the cheese in pieces instead, and dropped them on the path as he went along.

And so he came to where the neighbour was.

"I say, mister!" said the lad. "You'll have to be on the look out, for my master has discovered that my mistress asks you to our house when he is away, so now there'll be a fine kettle of fish."

And then he ran back to his master.

"Master!" he cried. "For God's sake, master, make haste and take the axe with you. Our neighbour has felled a big tree, which has fallen right across him."

"Dear, dear! What a misfortune!" cried the farmer; and set off running with the axe in his hand.

When the neighbour caught sight of him running towards him in this way he remembered what the lad had said, and took to his heels as fast as he could. The farmer stared after him in surprise; at the same time he was glad to see he was unhurt. "Wait a bit!" he cried. "Wait a bit, do you hear? I have got something nice for you over here."

Something nice? No, thank you; he was much obliged, but he thought it was best to keep away, for that kind of treat he could do without. He took to running still faster; he never said a word—he only ran.

"I should say he has gone mad," said the farmer; "for as a rule he does not want much pressing. But to run the flesh off your bones to get people to eat up your food when you're hungry, why, only a fool would do that," he said, and so he went back.

But then he saw the pieces of cheese which the lad had dropped along the path.

"What a careless boy!" he thought; and began to pick up the pieces as he went along.

In the meanwhile the lad was sitting beside his mistress, eating and drinking and gorging himself from the bag.

"What's father picking up over there?" said the woman.

"Pebbles," said the lad.

"Pebbles?" said the woman. "What is he going to do with them?"

"How should I know?" said the lad. "But you had better take care, mistress, for my master knows how you carry on with our neighbour when he is away. He knows it was for our neighbour, and not for him, that you brought this dinner; and now there'll be a nice kettle of fish."

The woman, as you may guess, turned red and became quite frightened.

"Heaven help me! heaven help me!" she muttered; and then she set off homewards.

The farmer shouted after her; but she would not hear him—she only ran as fast as she could.

"I think she is gone mad as well," he said; "or what is it she is running after?"

"Indeed, I don't know," said the lad; "unless the house is on fire."

"You don't say so!" shouted the farmer; and he took to his heels as well.

But his wife was more nimble on her legs, and she got home first. She ran into the kitchen and hid herself in the baker's oven. The farmer rushed to the well and filled a bucket with water, and ran into the kitchen. But he could see no fire anywhere.

"MY DEAR, KIND HUSBAND! DON'T BE ANGRY WITH ME!"
SHOUTED THE WOMAN.

"I wonder if it's in the baker's oven!" he said; and opened the door and threw the whole bucket of water into it. The wife began to shout and cry: "My dear, kind husband! Don't be angry with me! I will never ask our neighbour here any more when you are out, and I'll never take him any food either."

"Ah ha!" said the farmer. "Is that how matters stand? It's no wonder then that you have nothing but water-gruel for me! Did ever one hear the like? But I'll not stand it any longer; no, I'll not stand it!"

And he dragged his wife out of the oven and began to beat her as hard as he could.

The wife cried and screamed, but all of no avail; the more she screamed the more he belaboured her, for now he was fairly started.

Just then the lad came in.

"I think you had better take a rest now, master," he said; "for I suppose you have been thanking mistress for the grand feast."

"You think so?" said the farmer. "No—o! She must have more!" And so he wanted to begin again.

"No, stop!" said the lad; "it's enough now."

"Is it?" said the farmer. "I suppose it'll have to do then. But I haven't let him have anything yet."

"You mustn't either," said the lad.

"Mustn't I? Yes, indeed I will; and in such a way that I'll break every bone of that rascal's back."

"No, indeed you mustn't," said the lad. "I'll manage him."

"Will you?" said the farmer; and he did not at all object to this, for he had seen sufficient to know that the lad was able to manage it better than he, and that it was no joke when any one got into his clutches.

"Well, you had better do it, then!" he said.

So the lad went to the neighbour.

"Good evening!" he said.

"Good evening! How are things going?" said the neighbour.

"Very badly," said the lad; "for I must tell you that master is sharpening his axe, and is so furious with you that if you don't take care of yourself you'll never know what will happen. He has sworn he'll cut those shanks of yours to bits because you carry on with his wife when he is away."

"Oh dear, oh dear! What a scrape I have got into! What can a wretched man like me do?"

"Well, you must listen to what I say," said the lad; "you see, they have scarcely any corn left at our place and if you will give me two barrels of rye, half a barrel of peas, and a quartern of wheat, I shall be able to keep him quiet."

"Are you mad? So much for so little?"

"How do I know if it's too much or too little?" said the lad; "but I'll ask your wife about it, and then we shall soon know."

"No, stop!" said the farmer. "My wife, you see, has such a hasty temper. But one barrel of rye I might be able to manage, if only she doesn't get to hear of it."

"Two barrels," said the lad.

"One barrel," said the farmer.

"Two," said the lad, "or else——"

"No, no! stop! You shall have them then."

But the lad was not yet satisfied. He wrangled and bargained so long that he got the quartern of wheat, but of the peas he could only get half of what he wanted, for else they would run out of pease-meal altogether. The other quartern he would owe him. The lad was satisfied with this; and he was to come at midnight to fetch the corn, so that the neighbour's wife should not know anything about it; and with this they parted.

When the lad came back the farmer asked him: "Well, have you given him what he deserved?"

"Yes, you may be sure of that," said the lad. "He has now got enough to make his back smart for some time to come, and more he may get whenever I have a chance. But this you must keep to yourself, and you mustn't let either him or any of his notice anything. You understand that? And not a word to mistress either."

Yes, that the farmer promised.

"I say, master," said the lad, "I think you have now taught mistress to be obedient and to look after the crumbs better; but she has scarcely a morsel in the house, so I will be off to the mill, so that she can get her barrels and bins filled."

"To the mill?" said the farmer. "What are you going to grind? We have scarcely anything else but siftings in the bins."

"Oh, I'll see to that," said the lad. "Go to bed, and don't trouble about it."

"That's a wonderful lad!" thought the farmer. And then he did as the lad had told him; but the lad went into the cart-house and greased the wheels of the cart and got ready to start. In the middle of the night he called at the neighbour's for the corn, and then he drove to the mill.

But we know what womenfolk are. Even if they never go farther than from the hearth to the kitchen shelf they know what's going on in other people's houses for all that. And if they don't know they begin to wonder, and don't rest till they have found out. The neighbour's wife knew well enough how things were at the other farm, and when she heard they had taken on a servant lad, she wondered what they were going to give him to eat, and when she was told they had a cartload of corn at the mill, she began to wonder still more. Yes, she wondered and wondered, and could not rest till she had found out where they had got the corn from. She had her mother living with her—an old crone between eighty and ninety, or thereabout. But, old as she was, she was just as inquisitive as her daughter. And they kept on wondering so long till at last they hit upon a plan; and then the woman went to her neighbour.

"Good morning!" she said.

"Good morning!" said the farmer.

"We are all going to a party," she said, "and will you kindly let me leave a chest with you, while we are away? For I am rather anxious about the chest, I must tell you, as all the best we have is in it."

But the best was really her mother, who was hidden in the chest, and was to listen to what the people talked about. But nothing was said about this, of course.

"Oh, there won't be any difficulty about that," said the farmer; and so the woman and her servant girl carried in the chest, and then they set out for the party.

Soon afterwards the lad came back from the mill. And now his mistress had all kinds of flour, and she began to make both bread and pancakes.

All at once the lad saw the chest.

"What chest is that?" said he.

"Oh, it belongs to our neighbour," said the farmer. "They have gone to a party and have left it with us; for there is something very precious in it," he said.

"Ah, indeed!" said the lad. "I wonder what that can be? But I suppose we can have a look at it," he said; and so he took his axe and forced open the lid.

He then saw the old woman inside the chest.

"Hullo! Here's something precious indeed!" he said. "Just come and look!"

The farmer and his wife looked into the chest, and to their horror saw the old woman lying there as if she were dead.

"I think she is dead," said the farmer.

"And so do I," said the lad; "but we may as well try and see if there is life in her, or what can be the matter." And so he struck the side of the chest with his axe, to see if she would wake up and come to her senses.

But the old woman did not move a limb; she lay as stiff as a log.

Then he struck the chest again, but still she did not stir.

"Dead she is," said the lad; "but she must have come here alive, at any rate, for she has pancake and ham with her."

He took a piece of the pancake and put it in her mouth, whereupon he closed the lid again, so that no one could see it had been opened.

Later on the neighbour's wife came to fetch the chest, which she took away with her. Now she would get to know a lot of news, she thought, and she was quite looking forward to it.

But there was little occasion for joy, as you may imagine, when she opened the chest and found that her mother was dead, and had a piece of the pancake in her mouth.

"Oh dear! oh dear! She has been suffocated!" she cried. "Oh dear! how stupid I was not to give her as much as a drop of beer with her! Oh! what a misfortune!" and she cried and wailed till it was terrible to hear.

But what was done could not be undone, and since she could not cry life into the old mother, they would have to think of the funeral. And a grand funeral it should be; that was only fair and reasonable, in return for all her mother had suffered.

And this was done; the clerk chanted over the corpse till the walls creaked, and the parson preached about her life and good deeds till every nook in the church resounded with his words. The festivities were on the same scale; all the parish was there, with the exception of the lad, for they thought they had nothing to thank him for.

But the lad thought otherwise; and as he could not join in the eating and drinking, he thought he would find something else to do. He went to the churchyard about midnight and dug up the old woman, carried her in his arms and put her in the cellar among the beer barrels. The beer he carried across in pails to his master's cellar and poured it into his barrels, but the taps he placed in the old woman's hand, and then he went his way.

In the morning the neighbour's wife had to go to the cellar for beer, for the guests were thirsty, and wanted something to moisten their parched throats with. But you may imagine how terrified she was when she saw her mother sitting there.

"Oh dear! oh dear! That's because I left mother in the chest without giving her anything to drink," she said.

She ran to her husband, and he hurried to the parson to come and make his mother-in-law listen to reason. The parson told him to make his mind easy, and if he would promise to pay for a new funeral, he would read such prayers over the corpse that she would be sure to rest in her grave, said the parson; and the clerk would chant so that it could be heard all over the parish; and that would help a good bit too, added the clerk.

The new funeral took place on the following Sunday, and this time they did not forget the old custom of sewing the stockings together on the corpse and to put a thunderbolt in the coffin. Yes, they even put a whole bottle of beer beside her; and now they thought she could surely have nothing to look for in her son-in-law's house. And if the feasting wasn't greater, it wasn't at any rate less than at the first funeral; for everything was so grand that the old woman ought surely to rest satisfied, they thought. And so she might perhaps, if only the lad had been asked to the feast. But they had not asked him this time either, and so he went to the churchyard and dug her up again and carried her back to the farm. He placed her in the pea-bin in the barn, with a corn shovel in each hand. The peas he took away with him, for there was scarcely more than the quartern which the farmer owed him, and so he went away, leaving the door wide open.

In the morning they saw the barn door was open, and the farmer went to see what was the reason. But he nearly went out of his mind when he saw his mother-in-law sitting in the pea-bin, and found what havoc she had made there. "Did you ever see anything like it? This time she wanted to pay us out for the pancake which choked her," he said. "It's quite impossible to please that woman."

But there she sat in any case; and since she would not take herself off, there was no help for it but to go to the parson again. He wondered greatly at the old woman, who would not take any notice of all they had read and chanted over her. But if the man would pay him double fees, he would read so many prayers over her that she must remain in her grave; "there could be no question about that," said the parson. And the clerk would have to get some assistance, and they would sing so that it would be heard over seven parishes; "and that would be sure to help," said the clerk. The third funeral then took place, and they had now taken every care that the old woman should remain where she was. Yes, the parson read, the clerk chanted, and all the relatives, both in and outside the parish, were asked to the funeral feast.

But when the devil is abroad, it's little use to bar and bolt, and the lad was not asked this time either.

Close upon midnight the farmer said to the parson: "I am afraid that my mother-in-law is not satisfied this time either! Won't you let me drive you to the church, so that you could read over her once more, and then she would surely be at rest?" The parson would rather be excused, for he was enjoying himself at the funeral feast; but the farmer begged and prayed so hard that the parson promised to go, and so they drove off. When they came to the churchyard, the lad had already been there and dug up the old woman, but he had not got further than behind the church, and there he sat in a corner with the body in his lap.

The moon was shining, and the farmer had a foal, which was frolicking about after the mare. While the parson was reading over the grave the lad got hold of the foal, and then he took a stake and fixed it to the old woman's back, so that she could keep upright, and then he placed her across the foal. When the parson had finished he and the farmer set out on their way back.

"Now I think your mother-in-law will rest where she is," said the parson; but the same moment the old woman rushed past as swiftly as an arrow on the foal's back. The parson stood aghast and did not know what to say, and the farmer was quite at his wit's end; neither the parson nor the clerk could manage her. All the guests were lost in wonder, and pitied the farmer all they could, but they could not give him any advice.

At last his neighbour said to him: "I think we'll have to send for my servant lad. He may be able to manage the matter, for he is never at a loss."

"Ah, but what can he do? Is he better than the parson and the clerk?" they all said. But the farmer was quite certain that his lad was not to be despised, and since there was nothing else to be done they might as well try what he could do. And so they sent for him, and he came.

"Can you tell me how I shall make peace with my mother-in-law?" asked the farmer.

"I should think I can," said the lad. "That's not a difficult matter. Let me have the old woman and I'll read so many prayers over her that she'll keep quiet for good," he said. "But I must have a hundred dollars for my trouble."

That was a lot of money, but if she would only leave him in peace it might not be so unreasonable after all, thought the farmer.

The lad then took the old woman and carried her to the churchyard and buried her; and as he did not dig her up again she remained where she ought to be.

And the people of the parish now began to say the lad was a far better hand at reading over the dead than the parson himself.

He got the hundred dollars; and he well deserved them, thought the farmer; for if it had not been for the lad his mother-in-law would have worried him into his grave, he declared. But he was anything but pleased about all the money he had had to pay the parson, for his chest was now cleaned out altogether.

From that time there was a change in the parish. The farmer who had been rich only just managed to keep things going, but the poor farmer got on well and prospered in everything, so that he was worth several hundred dollars more at the end of the year. This he had to thank the lad for; it was only the truth, and he should honestly reward him, he said.

But the lad was a wonderful fellow. He had a head of his own, and he would not have any payment for all the help he had given the farmer.

"A hundred dollars is sufficient payment for a servant lad," he said; "and I have got that from our neighbour, so you do not owe me anything."

"It's seldom you come across such a lad," said the farmer, who did not want to let him go.

"I think you must stop here another year," he said.

But the lad thanked him for his good offer; he could not stop any longer, he said.

"Why?" asked the farmer.

"Well, the parson has engaged me to help him," he said.

How he fared afterwards I have not heard; but if that lad has not become a parson, or a dean, or a bishop, then no one else has.

"ALL I POSSESS!"

There was once a farmer who was so stingy and close fisted that he could scarcely find it in his heart to eat anything; and as for giving anything away to anybody, that was quite out of the question. He also wanted to accustom his wife to do without eating, but it fared with her as with the pedlar's mare; she died from an over-dose of that doctrine, and so he had to find another wife in her stead.

And although he was what he was, there were plenty of girls who made themselves agreeable to him and were willing to begin where his wife had left off. For you must know he was rich, the ugly fellow, and it was his money they were after, although they knew they would have to suffer a little in return.

But he was not satisfied with any of them, for if they ate ever so little, they were sure to want something to eat. Those who were stout and comely would be too expensive to keep, and those who were thin and slender were sure to have a big appetite; so he was not able to find any one to his liking, although he had been all over the parish looking for one.

But the lad on the farm came to his assistance. He had heard of a girl in one of the neighbouring parishes, who was not even able to eat as much as a whole pea at one meal, but made it do for two.

The farmer was glad to hear of this; she was the girl he would like to have, and although she was somewhat deaf, so that she never heard more than half of what people said to her, he lost no time in proposing to the girl. Her father and mother said yes at once, seeing that the suitor was so rich, and it did not take him long to persuade the girl herself. A husband she must have some time or other, and so they clinched the matter, and the farmer entered into wedlock for the second time.

But after a time he began to wonder how his wife really managed to keep alive, for he noticed that she never took a morsel of food, or even drank so much as a drop of water, and this he thought was altogether too little. But she seemed to thrive very well for all that, and he even thought she was getting a little stouter.

"I wonder if she's deceiving me?" he thought.

So one day, when he was driving home from his work in the fields, he happened to meet his wife, who was coming from the cowshed with the milk.

"I wonder if she doesn't take a sip of the milk when she is straining it," he thought, and so he asked the lad to help him up on the roof and pull the damper aside, for he wanted to look down the chimney and see what his wife was doing. And this he did. He climbed up on the roof and put his head down the chimney, peering and prying all he could.

The lad then went in to his mistress.

"Master is now looking down the chimney," he said.

"Down the chimney?" said the wife. "Well, then you must put some faggots on the hearth and make a fire."

"I daren't," said the lad.

"If you daren't, I dare," said the woman, and so she made a fire and blew into it.

The farmer began shouting, for the smoke was nearly suffocating him.

"Bless me, is that you, husband?" said his wife.

"Yes, of course it is," said the farmer.

"What are you hanging there for?" she said.

"Oh, I was longing so much for you, wifey, that I went the shortest way," he said, and then he fell down on the hearth, and burned himself a good deal.

Some days passed and his wife neither ate nor drank, but if she did not grow stouter she did not become thinner.

"I wonder if she doesn't eat some of the bacon when she goes to the storehouse," he thought; and so he stole into the storehouse and ripped up one end of a large feather bed which was lying there. He crept into it and asked the lad to sew the ticking together again.

The lad did as he was bid, and then he went in to his mistress.

"Master is now lying inside the feather bed in the storehouse," he said.

"Inside the feather bed in the storehouse?" said the wife. "You must go and beat it well, so that neither dust nor moths get into it," she said, and so she took down a couple of stout hazel sticks and gave them to the lad.

"I daren't," said the lad.

"If you daren't, I dare," said the wife, and she went to the storehouse and began to beat the feather bed with all her might, so that the feathers flew about, and the farmer began shouting, for the blows hit him right across his face.

"Bless me, is that you, husband?" said the woman.

"Yes, of course it is," said the farmer.

"What are you lying there for?" said his wife.

"I thought I would lie on something better than straw for once," said the husband. They then ripped open the feather bed, and when he came out the blood was still streaming down his face.

Some days then passed and the wife neither ate nor drank, but her husband thought she was growing still stouter and more cheerful than ever.

"The devil knows what's at the bottom of all this," he thought. "I wonder if she drinks the beer when she goes into the cellar?"

And so he went down into the cellar and knocked the bottom out of an empty beer-barrel, and then he crept into the barrel, and asked the lad to put the bottom in again. The lad did as he was bid, and then he went in to his mistress.

"Master is now lying in the beer-barrel in the cellar," said the lad.

"In the beer-barrel in the cellar?" said the wife. "You must fill it with boiling juniper lye, for it's getting sour and leaky," she said.

"I daren't," said the lad.

"If you daren't, I dare," said the wife, and so she began boiling juniper lye, and then she poured it into the barrel. The farmer began to shout, but she poured a whole kettleful into the barrel, and yet another after that.

The man went on shouting louder and louder.

"Bless me, is that you, husband?" said the wife.

"Yes, of course it is," yelled the farmer.

"What are you lying there for?" said his wife.

But the farmer was not able to give any answer. He only moaned and groaned, for he was terribly scalded, and when they got him out of the barrel he was more dead than alive, and they had to carry him to his bed.

He now wished to see the parson, and while the lad went to fetch him the wife began to prepare some tasty dishes and to make cheese cakes and other nice things for the parson, so that he should not go away with an empty stomach.

But when the farmer saw how lavish she was in preparing all the dishes he shouted still louder than when he was scalded:

"All I possess! All I possess!" he cried, for he now believed they were going to eat up everything he had, and he knew that both the parson and the clerk were people who could make themselves at home and make a clean sweep of the table.

When the parson arrived the farmer was still shouting:

"All I possess! All I possess!"

"What is it your husband is saying?" said the parson.

"Oh, my husband is so terribly good and kind," said the wife. "He means that I shall have all he possesses," she said.

"His words must then be considered and looked upon as an intimation of his last will and testament," said the parson.

"Just so!" said the wife.

"All I possess! All I possess!" cried the farmer, and then he died.

His wife then had him buried, and afterwards she went to the proper authorities about her husband's affairs. And as both the parson and the clerk could give evidence that the farmer's last words were that she should have all he possessed she got it all. And when a year was gone she married the lad on the farm, but whether after that time she was just as hard of hearing I have never heard.

KATIE GREY.

There were once upon a time a man and a woman who agreed so well together that a harsh word had never passed between them since the beginning of their married life; for whatever the husband did the wife thought right and proper, and everything that she did the husband thought the best that could be done. They had not much to manage with, so they had to be very careful, even with the crumbs; but no matter how black things looked, they were always happy and contented.

But envy seems to find her way into every corner, be it ever so humble, and if there is no one else who begrudges people living in peace Old Nick always tries to get his foot inside. So he lay in wait outside their house, wondering how he should be able to sow ever so little dissension there.

He tried in one way and he tried in another and he tried in every way; but although he was always hovering about the house they kept so well together that he could not find a single chink through which he could slip in, however small he made himself.

But what Old Nick himself cannot accomplish wicked women may manage. In the same neighbourhood there lived one called Katie Grey, who was one of the right sort. To her he went, and asked if she could set the old couple against each other.

That wouldn't be very difficult, she thought; and if only he would give her a new jacket and a petticoat with red and green and blue stripes she would be sure to manage it so that Old Nick himself should not be able to do it better. Well, Old Nick agreed to that, and so they parted.

Early next morning, as soon as the husband had set out for the forest, Katie Grey rushed off to see the wife.

"Good morning, and well met!" she said, making herself as pleasant as possible.

"Good morning!" said the wife.

"You have a very good husband, you have, haven't you?" said Katie Grey.

"Yes, the Lord be praised!" said the wife. "When the first snow falls this autumn it will be six and thirty years since we were married, and never during all these years has a single harsh word fallen from his lips."

Katie Grey quite agreed with her, as you may guess. "Yes, he is no doubt one of the best men one can meet in a day's walk," she said. "But I know people who have got on just as well as you two, and yet trouble came in the end."

"Poor people!" said the wife. "But just as soon will the mouse lie down with the cat, as such things will be heard about us," she said.

Well, that might be. Katie Grey was not one to believe all that people said, but "better wise beforehand than hasty afterwards," and "those who remedies know, can well kill illness, I trow;" and as she knew of a remedy against such a misfortune, she thought she ought to mention it, for when they had lived together like a pair of turtle doves for six and thirty years it would be both "sin and shame" if they were now to begin to bicker and quarrel.

The wife could not say anything to that.

"Well, you see," said Katie Grey, for now she thought she had got the better of the wife, "if you take a razor and draw it three times along a strop against the sun, and then cut off six hairs from your husband's beard just under his chin one night when he is asleep, and afterwards burn them, he will never be angry with you."

The wife said she did not think she would ever be in need of that remedy, but she thanked her for her good advice all the same.

Katie Grey then set out for the forest, where the husband was making osier-bands.

"Good morning, and well met!" she said.

"Good morning to you!" said the man.

"What a very kind and good wife you have got!" she said.

"That's true enough," said the man. "There isn't a better woman on this side of the sun, nor has there ever been one either."

"That may be," said Katie Grey, "but so was Eve also before the Evil One got the better of her."

"Yes, that's true; but my wife, you see, is not one of that sort, for she never puts her foot where such wickedness is going on," he said.

"Don't be so sure about that, for the Evil One can creep through the eye of a needle," she said, "so that no one is secure against him. Not that I want to make any mischief between people,—no one can say that about me,—but those who will run into danger had better be well looked after. 'All is not gold that glitters,' and 'outside mild, inside wild,' often go together," she said.[2]

"You talk according to the sense you have," said the man, who began to feel angry. "My wife is no more likely to wish me evil than the sun to shine in the middle of the night—that I may tell you," he said.

"NO, KEEP AWAY FROM ME!" CRIED OLD NICK, AND KEPT HER BACK WITH HIS POLE.

"Thinking and believing do no harm to anybody," she said. "But I think you will do a wise thing in not closing your eyes to-night when your wife comes and draws a razor across your throat. But not a word about this to any one, do you hear?" she said, and off she went.

One gets to hear a good deal before one has done with this world—but did one ever hear the like of this? Could it be possible? The man felt as strange in his head as if he had rolled down the church steeple; but whatever it was that ailed him, there he stood pondering and brooding.

Pshaw! She was after all only a wicked woman, who wanted to set them against each other. Yes, that was it; and he was very sorry he had not given her a good thrashing for her trouble.

But although he worked away and toiled his best with his osiers, he could not get out of his head what Katie Grey had put into it; and when he came home in the evening he was so depressed and silent that his wife had never seen him in such a state before, so strange was he.

"Goodness knows, what can be the matter with my husband?" she thought; and then she suddenly recollected what Katie Grey had told her.

"I may as well take three hairs from his beard," she thought, "for when you have had a happy home for six and thirty years, it isn't likely you'll let it slip through your fingers all at once." But she did not dare to speak to her husband,—she only asked him to lend her his razor.

He let her have it, but he sighed and thought to himself: "I wonder if she would do me any harm? I wonder if she really could? Oh, no! that's quite impossible."

But he put his axe close to his bed, and then they both lay down to rest.

Later on in the night she asked:

"Are you asleep, husband?"

This startled the man, but he did not say a word, and the wife stole out of bed and lighted a candle.

The man's heart began to beat violently.

The wife then took the razor and drew it three times along the leather belt of her husband's apron, and went towards the bed.

The blood rushed to the man's head, so that he almost lost his senses, but he lay as quiet as a stone, and only moved his hand towards the axe.

The wife then came close to the bed to cut the three hairs from his beard.

But as she leaned forward the man suddenly jumped up and seized his axe, with which he struck his wife, who fell down dead on the floor.

He felt he had done a very wicked deed, but he had not thought that things would come to this pass.

He became much distressed—for what was he going to do?

JUST THEN TWO WHITE PIGEONS CAME FLYING OUT OF THE
COTTAGE...THEY WERE THE MAN AND HIS WIFE.

It was perhaps best he followed his wife, and so he took a knife and
cut his throat.

Just then he heard some one laughing outside the window, and he
looked in that direction. There he saw Katie Grey, and then he died.

Katie Grey was now quite proud that she had been able to do more than the Evil One himself.

Old Nick was not far off either. He came with a petticoat and a jacket hanging on a long, long pole, which he held out towards her.

"Come nearer, so that I may shake hands with you and thank you," she said.

"No, keep away from me!" he cried, and kept her back with his pole, which he poked at her.

"You call me the Wicked One and the Evil One and such things, but I am not as wicked as you are, at any rate. Look here," he said, "take what belongs to you, so that I can have done with you." And with this he threw the pole and the clothes at her, and took to his heels as fast as ever he could, so afraid was he of her.

Katie Grey stood wondering and staring after him. Just then two white pigeons came flying out of the cottage, and flew right up into the clouds above. They were the man and his wife; for though Old Nick had wished them evil, the Lord would take care of them. But what would become of Katie Grey, seeing that the Evil One himself did not dare to go near her, it is not easy to say.

THE COCK AND THE CRESTED HEN

There was once a cock who had a whole farm-yard of hens to look after and manage; and among them was a tiny little crested hen. She thought she was altogether too grand to be in company with the other hens, for they looked so old and shabby; she wanted to go out and strut about all by herself, so that people could see how fine she was, and admire her pretty crest and beautiful plumage.

So one day when all the hens were strutting about on the dust-heap and showing themselves off and picking and clucking, as they were wont to do, this desire seized her, and she began to cry:

"Cluck, cluck, cluck, cluck, over the fence! cluck, cluck, cluck, over the fence!" and wanted to get away.

The cock stretched his neck and shook his comb and feathers, and cried:

"Go not there!" And all the old hens cackled:

"Go—go—go—go not there!"

But she set off for all that; and was not a little proud when she got away, and could go about pluming and showing herself off quite by herself.

"CLUCK! CLUCK!" SHE CRIED, AND WANTED TO GET AWAY.

Just then a hawk began to fly round in a circle above her, and all of a sudden he swooped down upon her. The cock, as he stood on top of the dust-heap stretching his neck and peering first with one eye and then with the other, had long noticed him, and cried with all his might:

"Come, come, come and help! Come, come, come and help!" till the people came running to see what was the matter. They frightened the hawk so that he let go the hen, and had to be satisfied with her tuft and her finest feathers, which he had plucked from her. And then, you may be sure, she lost no time in running home; she stretched her neck, and tripped along, crying:

"See, see, see, see how I look! See, see, see, see how I look!"

The cock came up to her in his dignified way, drooped one of his wings, and said:

"Didn't I tell you?"

From that time the hen did not consider herself too good to be in the company of the old hens on the dust-heap.

OLD NICK AND THE PEDLAR

There was once a pedlar who travelled all over the world with his bag on his back, and a yard measure in his hand. But he did not get on as well as other pedlars, for while they got rid of two or three bagfuls, he was not able to get one bag emptied.

So one evening, as he dragged himself wearily along the roadside, he happened to meet Old Nick, who was lying in wait; for since people had become so Christian, Old Nick had to content himself with pedlars, and such like.

"How is business?" asked Old Nick.

"Oh, times are very bad," said the pedlar. "Wherever I put my head in through the door, I find some of my mates have been before me, and the womenfolk will buy no more, and the men look angry," he said.

"Well, there's a remedy for that," said Old Nick. "If you will come to an arrangement with me you'll find that things will be different," he said.

Yes, the pedlar had no objection to that, for Old Nick would be sure to have him in the end at any rate; and so they made a bargain that the pedlar should sell all he bought, but if the bags ever became quite empty he should belong to Old Nick there and then.

That was a good bargain, thought the pedlar, for he would take care to manage it so that his bags never became quite empty; and then he set off home and got a horse and cart and goods of all kinds on credit. Then he drove from farm to farm and from one fair to another, and before long he had to go into town again for more goods. But however briskly business went, he always managed to have something left in his bags.

But Old Nick is not one to let anything slip through his fingers if he has once got hold of it, and so he followed close upon his heels, although the pedlar could not see him.

So one day he came to Hinnersmess fair, where there were crowds of people, and business was so brisk that it was as much as he could do to get out his stuff and measure what they wanted. For no doubt Old Nick had managed it so that his goods attracted the people's attention most.

There were other pedlars at the fair, of course; but neither words nor tricks were of any avail, for, in spite of all their gesticulations and persuasive ways, they sold little or nothing, as most of the people went to Old Nick's pedlar.

BUSINESS WAS SO BRISK, THAT IT WAS AS MUCH AS HE COULD DO TO GET OUT HIS STUFF AND MEASURE WHAT THEY WANTED.

In order to get some share of the business they had to sell their goods to him, and no sooner were they on his stall than they were sold there and then.

But a pedlar is also a human being, if not exactly one of the best sort; and although he was doing a brisk business he was obliged to leave his stall for a short time, and so he asked one of his mates to attend to his customers in his absence.

While he was away, a man came and asked how much the whole lot would cost, for he wanted to buy it all, and the horse and cart and the bags as well.

"Six hundred crowns," said the pedlar, for you see he thought he might be beaten down. But the man did not even try to bargain by as much as a penny; he put the money at once on the stall.

"And now it's all mine, you understand," he said; and then he laughed. "Tell your mate I shall come to-night to fetch the goods, and then we shall have a drink together on the strength of the bargain," he said; and then he laughed once more, and to such an extent that it sounded like thunder, and the next moment he was gone. It was easy to guess who the person was, for the whole market-place smelt of sulphur.

When the pedlar came back, he asked: "Have you sold anything?"

"Yes, of course I have," said his mate. "I have done a grand business, too! I have sold the whole lot, and the horse and cart, and the bags as well, for four hundred crowns; and here they are," he said, and gave them to him. But the other two hundred crowns he put in his own pocket, for he wasn't a pedlar for nothing, you see.

"The Lord have pity on me then, poor wretch that I am!" moaned the pedlar. "Now I am completely undone."

"Have you gone out of your senses?" said his mate. "He was one of the right sort, I can tell you. He did not even beat me down a stiver, and to-night he is coming to have a drink with you on the strength of the bargain."

"Oh dear, oh dear!" cried the pedlar; and he wailed and moaned so terribly that everybody pitied him, for they thought he had gone out of his mind.

Just then a woman came by.

"What is it you are crying and groaning about?" she asked. But the pedlar went on moaning, for now he felt there was no help for him.

"Be quiet!" said the woman; "don't go on like that, my man! It can never be so bad but it can be bettered, I say; for I am Katie Grey, [3] and I can always help people out of their trouble, even if it be Old Nick himself you have fallen out with," she said. "Come, let me only hear what's the matter, and we'll find a way out of it."

The pedlar then told her all about his trouble.

"If that was all," she said, "she would be able to help him, if he only did what she told him; which he, of course, was willing to do, as long as he could save his skin."

THE PEDLAR OPENED THE BAG, AND WHO SHOULD PEEP OUT BUT KATIE GREY!

When the night had set in Old Nick lost no time in coming to fetch him.

"You thought perhaps you could cheat me, but now you'll have to come with me after all," he said.

"There's no help for it, I suppose," said the pedlar; "but tell me, master, what did we arrange? Was it the whole lot you bought?" he asked.

"Yes, of course," said Old Nick; "I bought the whole lot, and horse and cart, and the bags too, and you remember the contract, I suppose?"

"Well, then, you bought what I have got here in this bag as well," said the pedlar, pointing to a great big bag which stood in a corner.

"Yes, it's all mine," said Old Nick. "But what sort of goods have you got in that bag? It looks so strange!"

"It's the best of all I have," said the pedlar, and opened the bag, and who should peep out but Katie Grey!

But then Old Nick opened his eyes and gave a start like a scared hare.

"Whew!" he shouted. "I haven't bought that bag, for any one who knows that fiendish creature would not have her as a gift."

"Yes, but then you haven't bought all of it," said the pedlar, "for she is mine as well, and she must go with the lot," he said.

"No, thank you!" said Old Nick. "I can easily do without a pedlar, for there are more of them; but if I take Katie Grey into the bargain I shall never have any peace. I know that terrible creature," he said.

With that he released the pedlar from his bond, and flew up through the chimney, carrying off the roof with him.

What happened afterwards I have never been able to find out; but if Old Nick could not get on with Katie Grey, the pedlar is not likely to have been any the better by the exchange either.

WHY THE EXECUTIONER IS CALLED ASSESSOR

Many, many years ago—well, it's so very, very long ago that no one can really tell how long ago it was—a number of grandees entered into a conspiracy against the king. But in spite of their power and arrogance he succeeded in laying them by the heels, and those who were not willing to swear submission to him there and then were all to lose their heads, which was only fair and just; for if one has not got more sense in one's head than to engage in such foolish undertakings, one may as well do without a head.

But since they were all such grand folks, the king himself wanted to see that everything was carried out properly; and so he set out for the spot where the execution was to take place, which was some distance away in the country. The executioner was, of course, going there as well; but he was not then such a great personage as he is now, and did not travel in such state, either at the public expense or at his own. Oh no, he had to trudge and plod along on his own legs, were the distance ever so great.

So it happened that he got into the middle of a big forest just as night was setting in, and as there was no sign of any house where he could get lodgings, he looked about for a place where he could lie down and rest. But while he was walking about looking for one, he saw some smoke rising out of the earth, and then he discovered in the ground a trap door covered with turf. If the smoke had not been coming out through the chinks he would never have noticed it.

While he stood wondering where the smoke came from, the trap door was lifted up, and the sooty and dishevelled head of a woman appeared in the opening.

"Bless the man!" said the woman, "have you lost your senses, standing there staring like that? The robbers will be home directly, and if they see you they'll pay you out for prying about here, and you'll never hear the cuckoo again," she said, and then she disappeared into the ground again.

The executioner was not easily frightened, but, 'he who does take care, will always safest fare;' and so he quietly slunk away.

But as he trudged along he marked the trees with his axe; for 'when one knows where the wolf lives, one need not go to the furrier for his skin,' he thought.

So by dint of walking and running he came at last to his destination; and what he had come there to do he did so satisfactorily that he was well rewarded, and the king himself thanked him for his able assistance. But since the king was so condescending as to speak to one whom other people would not be seen with, the executioner thought he might as well have his say also, and so he told the king what he had seen in the forest. The king was greatly pleased to hear of this, for these robbers had done so much mischief to him and other folks that he would like to get hold of them.

"If I could only get some people to come with me," said the executioner, "I should be sure to catch them, for now I know where they are."

"Yes, that was all very well," thought the king; but he wanted to do this business in his own way, for he was strong and bold beyond all bounds. He was so powerful, indeed, that no one ventured to wrestle with him, for he could throw one and all to the ground in less than no time.

"What do we want with people?" he said. "If you will only come with me and show me the way, I think we two might venture a bout with them," he said; "for you look no weakling either."

Well, the executioner had no objection to that, for it wasn't every day he was in such company, and so they settled how they should set about it.

The king took off his crown and all his finery, and then they dressed themselves up like the worst of tramps, and blackened their faces and tore their clothes into pieces, so that the rags hung and dangled about them. The king put a sword inside his trousers, and the executioner hid his axe under his jacket; and so they set out.

No sooner had they got into the forest than they met the robbers, of whom there were altogether twelve.

"Who are you?" asked he who seemed to be their chief.

"We are a couple of miserable wretches, who are obliged to beg our bread," said the executioner. "We haven't tasted a morsel the whole day, and don't know what we are going to do for the night either," he said.

"There isn't much to be got out of you, poor beggars!" said the robber; "but that makes no difference. Since you have got into the forest you'll have to die, and no mistake," he said.

"God bless you for your pretty speech!" said the executioner, looking as miserable as he possibly could. "How lucky we were to fall in with you, for you know very well it's no pleasure to live when your stomach groans for food, and when you cannot get a morsel to satisfy it with. But since you are such a mighty lord, you might give us a good feed first, for, after all, it's hard to die on an empty stomach."

"FOR, AFTER ALL, IT'S HARD TO DIE ON AN EMPTY STOMACH,"
SAID THE EXECUTIONER.

This greatly amused the robber, who laughed; and then the others began to laugh, so that their laughter could be heard all over the forest.

"Have you never had a good feed, poor wretches?" he asked. "Well, I'll be extravagant for once in my life. So come along, and you shall have as much as you can put into your carcases. But to tell the truth, nobody who falls in with me, need trouble much about food for the rest of their life," he said; and so he laughed, and then the other robbers laughed till the forest trembled.

They then set out for the robbers' cave, and there they lifted up the trap-door, and slid down under the ground one after the other, and the two tramps as well.

There was a large room down there, and a long table in the middle, which stood ready laid. The woman with the sooty face carried in the food on silver dishes to the robbers, who sat side by side on the bench along the wall. They feasted and drank burnt brandy out of large chalices, and talked and bragged about all their valiant deeds, while they were having their fill.

When the robbers had had enough both of food and drink, the tramps were allowed to sit down to the table, but on the opposite side to the robbers.

The woman put both beef and pork before them, and each of them got his cup filled with brandy. But no sooner had she placed the food on the table than matters took quite a different turn. They planted their feet firmly on the ground, and pushed the table with such force against the robbers, that they were fixed against the wall as if they were nailed to it. Then they threw the brandy into the robbers' eyes, and the king drew forth his sword and the executioner his axe, and before the robbers could rub the brandy out of their eyes they were all killed.

This was a big capture, and no mistake; and the king was greatly pleased with it. All that was found in the robbers' cave he wanted to give to the executioner; but "no thank you," he answered, "there was something else he would like to have."

"Well, what might that be?" asked the king.

"Well, your majesty," he said, "if an executioner becomes ever so rich he's always looked upon as a butcher; and the people spit after him just as if he were a knacker or Old Nick himself, and he is hardly ever allowed to mix with respectable people, however honest he may be. I would therefore most humbly ask your majesty to ordain it so that an executioner shall be respected like other people," he said.

"Yes, that is fair and reasonable," said the king; "and so it shall be."

The king accordingly issued an edict that no one must dare to spit after the executioner, for his calling was just as respectable as any other; and in order that no one should be ashamed to be in his company he was to have the title of Assessor, and wear a three-cornered hat when he was in full dress. Such was the edict, and so it is to this day.

But as the executioner would not accept what the robbers had hoarded, the king gave it to the woman who had served with them; and when she had combed the hair away from her eyes and washed the soot off her face she turned out to be quite a handsome woman. The executioner then thought that as the king had been so generous to him he would not be behindhand either, and so he made her the Lady Assessor; and thus after all he became possessor of all that the robbers had hoarded up.

THE PARSON AND THE CLERK

There was once upon a time a parson who was such a miser that he even begrudged the beggars a meal; and as for giving a poor fellow a shelter for the night, he would not hear of it.

But he was a great preacher; and when he had once begun he would shout and thunder and strike the pulpit with his fists so that every corner in the church rang with his words. And his parishioners had nothing to complain about in this respect; but they did not like his meanness, and they thought it was a shame they had to put up with such a parson.

The parson's wife suffered not a little in consequence; for she was a kind and good woman, but she could do nothing with her husband.

Just before Christmas, when the poor were most importunate, the parson used to dress himself up like a tramp and sit in the kitchen in the evenings; and when some poor fellow came and asked for shelter for the night, the parson's wife had to say that they already had one to find room for, and would then tell him to go to the clerk, who was their nearest neighbour. The clerk, as you may guess, would have been just as pleased if he had not been troubled with these guests; for he thought—as was only too true—that it was more the parson's duty than his to feed and shelter the poor. But the clerk was a sly dog and full of fun and mischief, as parish clerks generally are.

It would be a strange thing, he thought, if there were not a remedy for meanness as well as for other ailments; so one evening, shortly before Christmas, he dressed himself like a tramp, and went to the parsonage and asked for shelter for the night.

Yes, that he should have had with pleasure, but they already had a stranger in the house, said the parson's wife, pointing to the other tramp, who was sitting by the hearth—for, of course, she never said a word about him being the parson. As matters stood she thought he had better go to the clerk, for they were not likely to have any strangers over there.

"Haven't they?" said the clerk. "Why, they have their place so full they have scarcely any room for themselves; for I have just come from there," he said, "and I don't think you would like me to sleep in the fields and freeze to death, would you?"

Oh, dear no, it wasn't likely; she could not be so unchristian; but as she had no place to put him she could not very well do anything for him, she said.

"I think you can," said the clerk; "if you can shelter one you can shelter two, and I don't suppose that this mate of mine is going to sleep in the parson's bed, is he?" he asked, and slapped the parson so hard on his back that he nearly tumbled on the hearth.

"We must be content, and be thankful as well, whichever way the world treats us," said the parson.

"What you say is quite true," said the clerk; "and I'll be quite content, and share the bed with you, if the lady of the house allows it, and she will then shelter two men to-night instead of one. For there is no help for it, as far as I can see," he said.

The parson's wife resisted his importunities as long as she could, for she thought the tramp would not be a pleasant bedfellow for her husband; but the clerk would by no means listen to her, so she had to give in at last.

They were to sleep in the servant lad's room in the brew-house, as he was away at the mill—the parson in the settle bed, and the clerk on the bench.

That was her order; but the clerk was not satisfied with the arrangement, and when he came into the room he threw himself into the settle-bed, and the parson had to content himself with the bench.

Before long the clerk stole out of the room, and when he came back he woke the parson and said:

"I have served out that miserly parson, I can tell you! I have made a hole in the loft of his wood-shed, so that all the corn he had stored in the room above is running down among his stacks of wood."

"Oh dear! oh dear!" wailed the parson.

"What's the matter with you?" said the clerk.

"I feel so bad, so bad!" said the parson, and off he ran to the wood-shed.

"I think I have given him something to do now, and why should I lie on this wretched straw? I shall find better quarters in the house," thought the clerk; and so he went into the house and sat down in the parlour by the fire. The door was open to the parson's bedroom, and in order that the wife should think it was her husband who had come in he imitated the parson's voice.

"I have been lying so uncomfortably," he said in a pitiful voice, "for that scamp of a tramp made me lie on the bench, so I thought I would come here and rest for a little while."

"Of course, of course, my dear," said the wife. "But why should you be so hard-hearted with people? It is a sin and a shame, that it is,—and it brings you no happiness either."

"Ah well, that may be," said the clerk, all the time imitating the parson. "I have been suffering so much to-night that I shall be better after this."

"God bless you for those words!" said the parson's wife.

In a little while the clerk said: "I must go now to that tramp, so that he does not find out where I am."

And off he went, and only just managed to lie down in time before the parson returned.

The parson had in the meantime been hard at work in the wood-shed trying to stop the hole in the loft, and had fallen head over heels many times among the logs and firewood, before he succeeded in doing so; but by that time nearly all the corn had found its way down into the wood-shed. He came back to the servant-lad's room puffing and groaning like a smith's bellows, and lay down on the bench. As soon as the clerk saw that he had settled down and got the blanket over his head, he stole out of the room again.

When he came back he woke the parson and said:

"I have now served the parson a still better trick. When I came outside and heard the wolves howling over the hills, I went into the cow-house and let out all the cattle."

"Oh dear! oh dear!" shouted the parson, and started as if he had been shot.

"What's the matter with you?" said the clerk.

"I feel so bad, so bad!" said the parson; and the next moment he was gone.

"I think you'll have enough to do for a long while now," said the clerk; and so he went back to the parlour.

"Are you there again?" asked the parson's wife from the bedroom.

"Yes, my dear," said the clerk, imitating the parson's voice. "I have sent that tramp on a fool's errand; and I have been suffering so much on the bench that I thought I would come here and rest again for a while."

"Yes, my dear, that you must," said the wife; and the clerk settled down in the chair by the fire.

In a while the clerk said; "I must go back to that tramp again, so that he does not find out where I am;" and then he went back to his bed.

In the meanwhile the parson had been running about the fields and the hills, and had fallen several times on his face, while he rushed about calling and driving in the cattle. He had a terrible struggle to get all the beasts back to the cow-house, for he had a large herd of cattle.

The clerk had not been long in bed when the parson came rushing into the room, puffing and groaning, so that one could not help pitying him; for he seemed to have lost his breath altogether.

"You were long away this time," said the clerk. "But in the meantime I have served out that miserly parson once more."

"What's that you say?" said the parson, who began to feel so ill at ease that he could scarcely keep on his legs.

"Yes," said the clerk; but this time he did not speak the truth. "I have been down in the cellar; and I have poured two buckets of ditch water in the beer barrel in the far off corner, for I thought the parson ought to have something to give his clerk at Christmas."

"Oh dear! oh dear!" shouted the parson.

"What's the matter with you?" asked the clerk.

"I feel so bad, so bad!" said the parson.

"Yes, I can imagine that," said the clerk; "and I pity you so much that now you may lie in my bed. It'll soon be morning, and I must be getting away. I don't expect I shall get any breakfast from this miserable parson, do you? Well, good-bye, then," he said; and off he went.

"Phew!" sighed the parson. He felt as if the whole parish had been lifted off his back; and no sooner was the clerk gone than he dragged himself in to his wife.

"Are you there again, husband?" she said.

"A-gain?" said the parson; it was with the greatest difficulty he was able to speak, so exhausted was he.

"Yes; you have been here twice before during the night," said his wife.

"Tw-ice?" groaned the parson.

"Yes, of course," said his wife.

"You have been dreaming!" said the parson.

"Oh dear, no; I don't dream when I don't sleep," said his wife. "But, my dear good husband, don't play such pranks another time!"

"No-o!" said the parson. "Better to give to the poor than to go through such misery as I have done to-night," he said, forcing the words out; and then he fell asleep.

All at once he started up and shouted to his wife: "My dear!"

"Well, my dear?" said his wife.

"The beer barrel in the furthest corner you must send to the clerk," he said.

"Bless my soul, but that's too much," said his wife.

"It's just—about right," moaned the parson; and then he fell asleep again.

Next morning the wife had the barrel of beer sent across to the clerk's house. He was much pleased to receive it, and sent back his thanks for it; for he knew the beer had not been tampered with. But the parson had the greatest trouble to sort out the corn from the splinters and rubbish in the wood-shed. But they kept on cleaning and shaking and sorting so long that at last they saved all the corn, with the exception of a few barrels.

But the parson never forgot that terrible night. He was cured of his meanness, and became quite a different person. He never refused any poor people either food or lodgings; and when the farmers came to pay their tithes in the autumn he gave them such a grand feast that his parishioners said they could never have wished for a better parson.

It was indeed worth a barrel of beer to have such a parish clerk!

RICHARD CLAY AND SONS, LIMITED, LONDON AND DUSGAY.

FOOTNOTES

[1] Any one led astray by the Huldre (the fairy of the wood of the North) must, according to popular belief, turn his jacket inside out three times before he can find his way.

[2] Under the name of *Titta*, or *Katie Grey*, there appears in many Swedish legends a witch of the worst kind, but still perfectly human in form. In her popular tradition has desired to personify that malice, coupled with cunning, which was likely to be found in a wicked woman, while at the same time it has endeavoured to show that before such a one even the prince of darkness must tremble.

[3] See the story, "Katie Grey."

THE END

26774619R00061

Printed in Great Britain
by Amazon